THE NIGHTCLERK

THE NIGHTCLERK:

Being His Perfectly True Confession

by Stephen Schneck

Grove Press, Inc. / New York, N.Y.

DEDICATED
TO THE ONE

THE NIGHTCLERK

fectly wonderful feeling that came from merely watching Lady K. walk across the tower room. It was delicious. She was crippled to such an extent that it took a four-and-a-half-inch platform on her left shoe to compensate for her short left leg.

The Baron nodded and she advanced, coming toward him with a peculiar and graceful rolling motion. With each step she would dip sharply forward, throwing her large breasts into prominence, and making her hips jut out at odd and exciting angles.

The veins bulged on the Baron's forehead. He slowly ran his eyes up her lush body. She cringed. Poor, helpless, hopeless Lady K. She knew only too well what she could expect. She was the Baron's favorite prisonerette. She was the Scapegoat, the woman he would send for when he wanted

"... a room? Hey, what do you say, mister? Let's have a little action here ..."

(DINGDINGDING!)

A meaty paw pounded the service bell, but no bellboy jumped for the luggage that wasn't there.

"C'mon, mister, don't you want to rent a room to me and my gorgeous l'il wife ... ?"

(DING?)

Behind the counter, seated at the roomdesk, an enormous toad looked up from his storybook and, without much interest, regarded the beefy, middle-aged, bell-pounding fool. One of the Regulars, trooping through the night, through the strip joints and amusement arcades and bars full of whores: half-hour wives at ten, twenty, and twenty-five dollars a trick.

(DING! DING!)

One of those tricky, quicky ladies was waiting at the side of this ding-a-ling Trooper. And only a drunken, cockeyed Trooper would have called her gorgeous. In truth, she was

9

nearly ugly enough to pass for a sin. Skinny as a wraith, with stringy red hair cut too short, and her nose too long, and very crooked. A nose that had been broken more than once. Only her mouth saved her. A fascinating mouth, a wicked mouth with delicious, carmine lips. Her voice was a rasp, and she used it to poke her clod. "Honey, get off of that Goddamned bell!"

A weary wink and a helpless shrug were her apologies to the Nightclerk.

He scratched his thighs for a good, long minute before he accepted them.

"I suppose, as a special favor, I could find you folks a double for about twelve, twelve and a half. . . ." He supposed he could do favors like that all night.

"The guy hasn't got but five to spend on the room, Spenser," the red-headed woman whined winsomely, her lips puckered furiously. "I certainly would appreciate it if you could give us some kind of room for a nickel. Spenser, sweetie, I swear to God, we wouldn't take long. . . ."

A Nightclerk gets paid by the hour. Personally, he's in no great rush. But how these hurry-up couples squirm!

Seated comfortably, altogether at his ease, Spenser studies them, considers their plight, and increases their tension a few pounds at a time.

This Nightclerk, an extraordinarily gross man of meticulous ritual, dispassionately observes while he searches himself with fat thumb and index finger, pinching around in the pockets of his stained, half-buttoned vest. And he won't say a word, nor give them a sign, till at last he's found his little gold snuffbox. Then he smiles. He has long, yellowed teeth.

"Did you want an *entire* room for that five?" the Nightclerk wondered, and his gaze met hers. They held hands with their eyes, while Blight tripped on blithely. "A whole room, with a bed and sheets and a pillow, a complete room, waste-basket, wallpaper, window, even an ashtray . . . ? Yes, you two look like the kind of people who smoke in bed. . . . But you say you can only pay me five poor dollars?" Blight gave his atten-tention to the bright, flat snuffbox, open in his palm. Deftly he pinched some cocoa-colored dust from box to yawning, suca-cious nostril. He inhaled extravagantly,

Aaaaaa . . .   Aaaaa . . .   Aaaaaaa HOOOOO!

Spenser cleared his sinus passages and six feet away, across the counter, the Trooper's necktie fluttered in the breeze.

"Ah good," Blight muttered, tears in his eyes. Shifted in his chair and searched for his nose rag. Now his eyes return to the girl. "Alright, Wanda, I'm going to do it. And I'll even throw in a door on this room, no extra charge!"

The Nightclerk weighed five hundred and twenty-nine pounds: he came out of his swivel chair, not like a fat man standing up, but like a whale climbing out of the sea. He rolled the three steps from desk to counter and plucked the five dollar bill from the Trooper's fingers just as that clown was drawing back, awestruck. He was a regular fool, but this was his first time at the Travelers. He'd never seen anyone, anywhere, like Spenser, not so close up.

The Nightclerk's smile grew even wider. He slid a key across the countertop. The Trooper was staring. Blight stared back. Very, very deliberately, looking the Trooper right in the eye, Blight licked his lips. The Trooper, the silly boy, saw the pink, forked tongue and he blanched, hurriedly looked else-where.

The deskpen and room register at the end of the counter. "Get away from there!" the Nightclerk bellowed.

The Trooper jumped, guilty as hell. "Not for a dirty, little old five, you don't sign," said Spenser, as though signing were really the best part of renting. "Go along," he grunted,

pocketing the bill. "Room three-o-one. I'll handle the register-
ing, you two go have fun." He inclined his head, huge, completely bald, towards the elevator. "Don't you be up there all
night, now, Wanda," he issued final words of warning before
sinking back into his custom-built swivel chair.

Leather cushions groaned shamelessly as his great weight
squeezed the air out of them. The wheels squeaked as Blight
leaned back, book in hand. He found his place just as the
elevator doors closed with a long and sibilant hisssssssss. . . .

". . . gloated over her adorable, but not quite ripe . . ."

the Nightclerk read to himself, while around him the immense
lobby began to fill up with ragged shadows. Inopportune, ex-
hibitionistic shadows. They whispered and giggled and plucked
at Blight's clothes. They ran their thin hands between his fat
thighs. Blight grunted and scratched, but he refused to look
up from his book, on principle.

". . . in case Mimi, the maid, should be about."

And the shadows washed over the great-domed skull . . .
but not even the shadows could be certain . . . only someone
sitting in Blight's lap would be able to tell whether or not his
eyes were open. Blight's bald head told nothing, nothing at
all. Without waiting to be asked.

Down at the end of town, at the bottom of Market Street,
the monstrous Travelers Hotel occupies a full city block. A
very special, zoned-off city block, outside the laws of nature as
well as most municipal ordinances. There are things that happen in this hotel, things for which there are no explanations.
Things that wouldn't look very good on the Record.

Fortunately, few records are kept.

And he who writes his name in the Travelers' register
signs on water. The pseudonymous and transient tribes of
Smith, Jones, Johns, Brown, White and Gray have left veracity

no room on the page. Reality has been crowded off the register. Names are regularly changed to protect the guilty.

> *Ask me no questions*
> *And I won't have to tell you*
> *any lies.*

is the unwritten house rule. No need for it to be embossed on the simulated leather cover of the spurious register that lay, its paper arms stretched wide open like a broad invitation to pen a lie, there on the counter beside a plaque, eight inches long, three inches high.

J. SPENSER BLIGHT

Nightclerk

---

and it was hardly necessary to add, Keeper of the Booke of Aliases, Booke of the Furtive 5 & 10 Dollar Lovers, Booke of the Total Losers. Book of those who register to do that to which they do not wish to sign their names.

In keeping with this guilt-charged atmosphere, the Nightclerk's plaque may be reversed:

ABSOLUTELY NO CHECKS CASHED

THE MGT.

One of the three undeviating sentiments at the Travelers Hotel. No Credit. No Questions. No Favors.

All night long, at the edge of that dim wasteland of a lobby, the Nightclerk scissors photographs out of magazines, and tends to the irregular traffic of Troopers, who stumble, venal and drunken, and sick at heart, their heads crowned with ashes. They bring their crimes across the great expanse of mildewed carpet, to stand, some belligerent, some trembling, some simply stunned by the enormity of the thing. All of them naked in front of the Nightclerk's counter, explaining the problem to J. Spenser Blight.

Rent a lady? Spug-a-mug? Pint of after-hour's whiskey? Two ladies? Two pints? Certainly. This is a free country, and as long as you can pay for it, you may have it. Pay now, please . . . yes sir, and here's your key and there's the elevator. Room 525, that's the fifth floor and to your left. . . . I'll send your wife up as soon as I can find one," Blight checks another one in. "Won't be but a couple of minutes wait," yawns Blight, who has been waiting for years. "Only be a few minutes, the girls are in and out of here all night. Go on up, I'll pick you a pretty . . ."

A pretty in and out, a pretty up and down. And oh but it's a long Blight till morning. Both the Nightclerk, and the hotel that he clerks in, are dying of repetition. They are drifting together, in the night; drifting out of life and into legend. Like stories told too often, they are exceeding the limits of plausibility; very soon they will be entirely gone into fantasy.

More and more guests are beginning to complain that while they sleep the hotel rises from itself, one image ballooning out of the other.

There are even some few persons who have gone so far as to suspect that this hotel, confined neither to space nor time, has entrances and exits on every dimension. They would have it that there exist five, six, seven hotels, all called the Travelers, and each one suspended above the other. A fantastic notion! But, if it were true . . . ?

If it were true, then no man could ever be certain that he had entered the correct hotel. No man could ever be sure that he was not lodged in bogus quarters. Add to that the confusion of having registered under a false name . . . one begins to perceive that the traveler takes not only a roomkey in hand, but his life as well, when he accepts a nod from the Nightclerk and steps into the elevator. Self-service, naturally; one must press his own button.

And the elevator doors close with an apopemptic hiss . . . then does more than one nervous traveler feel the first pricklings. As the cage rises up the blind shaft, a terrible truth suddenly intrudes. A key tagged with a room number, a John Doe on the register, and a nod from a nightclerk prove absolutely nothing but faith in a disgustingly obese Nightclerk's promise of a room on the fifth floor. In other words, one realizes too late (too bad), that one is trapped in a cage, ascending to a hypothetical room, a projected room; very possibly, a room that exists only in the Nightclerk's imagination. . . .

. . . and if you were to shout, who would hear you? And if you screamed, who would care? Has anyone ever troubled to tabulate the number of persons who sign a hotel register, step into an elevator, and are never seen again?

> *See them shuffle along,*
> *Shuffle, step, and shuffle. . . .*

. . . shuffle, time-step
and shuffle, shuffle, shuffle, shuffle, shuffle
> Down Memory Lane . . .

Steeped in the heartbroken atmosphere of the thirties, the splendid, ruined lobby of the Travelers is hung with wreaths of stale cigar smoke. This lobby, a stage set that was meant to dazzle for a season, has been expecting the wrecker for ages. This huge hall . . . and yet who can say just how huge, with any degree of exactitude? What measure holds true in the light of these chandeliers shedding inconstant light, unnatural shadings? Illumination so murky that one *senses* rather than ever sees the exaggerated proportions; one *assumes* the existence of the ceiling, somewhere up there in those stratospheric heights. An assumption which reinforces the curious and recurrent point of fact, that the entire lobby of the Travelers Hotel, from unseen ceiling to the vague horizons that one *assumes* are walls of the lobby, the entire area was a matter of conjecture. Say that it was intuitively perceived, rather than visually defined. The sort of lobby where one found exactly what one thought he would find. And if those shapes were not built into the walls, well then, perhaps they weren't. Perhaps they were something else.

And to tell a bit more of the truth, wasn't the lobby something of a grand conspiracy? Shall we say, something in the nature of a collusion of objects and attitudes and illuminative emphasis of the least reliable sort? And so nothing could ever be identified, not *positively* identified. The potted palms, for example . . . a traveler had only to cry, "Look! Look at the potted palms." And the potted palm would at once rearrange itself into an umbrella stand, done in marvelous detail, and featuring five big black umbrellas, hanging upside down by their hooked tails, just like five black storybook bats, or do you insist further? Will you keep staring? What is it you are trying to see?

Under scrutiny, the umbrella stand, together with the umbrellas, goes up in five fingers of smoke, and a gentle, dazed wind plays old, blind porter, scattering the ashes through the lobby.

Of course it is only a trick, done with mirrors. Done with an extraordinary number of mirrors, hanging crookedly in every corner of the lobby. Gilt peeling off the frames, dust dimming the glass. Angled mirrors catch unexpected pinpoints of light;

flash of small bright lights blinking around the edges of the weird lobby, like voices calling to each other, voices faint, lost far out at sea.

Closer in, a congress of inanimate objects is, apparently, in session. Baronial chairs confer in hushed, serious whispers with jittering, spindly, useless and unused old cabinets. A Wendell Willkie campaign button, and dust, two dead flies, an ossified cough drop, and a fingerbone in fifty-six drawers, divided among nine cabinets, a serious investigator might have discovered, had anyone been investigating.

Flocks of odd-sized coffee tables, writing tables, little old lady end tables, loving couples after all these years. And through the pastoral lounge, placid hippos, the low-slung herd of ancient couches, broken-down, spavined, exhausted old furniture turned out to pasture in the Travelers lobby. And that corpulent shepherd at his vigil behind the roomcounter, what queer gossip has he not overheard as the divans, grazing heavily among the cuspidors and standing lamps, the cranes and upholstered dragons, their stuffing leaking out, and their secrets showing, were telling tales about the guests and employees? And one never doubts that the lies are most outrageous in those farthest parts of the lobby, where the light is weakest there the shadows are invariably boldest.

Regrettable that everything is so predictable.

Behind the roomcounter, hunched over his obsession; the magazine lies open on his dark lap; the big, shiny, newly sharpened scissors snickering in his hand. These are the tricks played night after night. The Nightclerk cuts out real girls, while over his head paper dolls are crumpled and tossed under the bed. Not that Blight was to blame. Nobody had ever suggested that posing the girls was part of his job. And was it his place to object? If so, just how does one go about raising an objection to the odd and uncomfortable positions they force the girls into these days? What more can a man do than apply himself with a surgeon's skill, with caution, with sharp scissors? And even so, accidents will happen. There is never enough light. And other circumstances, lamentable but beyond the pitiful powers of the most celebrated magicians to alter or defer.

The above should not be interpreted as inference that Blight, Spenser J., was either celebrated, or a magician. He was, as previously stated, a Nightclerk. He was a man, suspiciously fat that's perfectly true, but, nonetheless, only a man, On duty, alone at 2:00 A.M. in an immense hotel lobby. He was a senior employee, suitably enthroned in his custom-built, soft-cushioned, leather and foam-rubber swivel chair, swiveling through the long, repetitious procession of legless hours. Hours crawling past with heartbreaking tribes of mutilated minutes, sending delegations of crippled pigmies, sixty of them at a time. To be dealt with as Blight sees fit.

(And later he will be able to claim that he was only following orders; and within the strict and narrow letter of the law, he will be, of course, absolutely correct.)

The most common manner of approaching the Nightclerk is along one of the four tongues that traverse the extensive, queerly lit lobby from street door to roomcounter. Four long, straight strips of carpeting, royal purple, once upon a long ago time. They're faded now, bled to a pale, nearly bloodless pink and threadbare path that leads to Blight, a swollen Eminence ensconced at the point of intersection. The desklight breaks on his bald crown. His scissors lick voluptuous half-moons from the paper page; describe an exquisite and tortuous calligraphy. Or so it might appear, and appearances continue to mislead. . . .

. . . Blight shifts his bulk. A magazine lies shredded in his commodious and richly stained lap. His vest and jacket are no cleaner. Traces of snuff, gravy, coffee, mud, laboratory acids, semen, boiled milk. . . . Blight's sleazy blue suit is history written in discolorations, decorations, drippings of major import, dapplings and egg stains of intriguing design.

The Nightclerk is no less intriguing. If his parts are fascinating . . . what may be anticipated regarding his whole?

It may be said, without fear of much disagreement, that J. Spenser Blight was one of the most physically repellent men alive. Not only did he weigh six hundred and seventeen bilious pounds, but he was negligent in his toilet, rarely shaved more than one side of his sallow, bejowled face, let his fingernails grow grubby and untended. He changed his scent from pinewood to unclean socks as caprice moved him. The top button of his pants had not been fastened since the day he bought the suit, and his belly, gray hairs showing in the space between his shirt and unbuckled belt, spilled over even when he stood —which was but rarely. . . . To remark that Blight's appearance was carefully calculated to give offense is to make a shaky, subjective judgment based entirely upon external evidence. One cannot be cautioned too often against this dangerous and inadmissible practice which has condemned more quasi-innocent men than any other only human failing. Nothing is what it seems to be. Therefore, the Nightclerk is neither fat, nor filthy; but playing a double game. At least. Three games is more likely. Else why such circumspection? Why such elaborate disguises? Why six hundred and twenty-six pounds? Enough (and more) to impress an eye of Captain Click's caliber—Capt. Click, formerly the hotel's most respected House Detective, a Scout Leader on his days off. Click—who had the happy knack of summing up a subject that has been under his surveillance with a brilliantly chosen sentence or two—in regard to Blight, observed that the only thing in downtown Frisco that was seedier than the Travelers Hotel was the hotel's Nightclerk, J. Spenser Blight.

(For his part, let the record stand that Blight never took umbrage at Click for his outspoken, and oft-spoken, humorisms and jocular recitations of Blightics. All monotonously obscene, and all constructed with Blight as the butt of Click's fiction, with Blight as the patron saint of Click's wit. Through all this sportive nonsense, Blight, who hated having his name bandied about in barbershops and cigar stores—where else could a man of Click's coarseness find cronies?—never reproached, remonstrated, or in any way gave notice that he was offended. Not even when Click took to addressing him as "Tubby!")

And when Click was arrested on four counts of Homosexual Paradoxy, Pederasty, Fondling the Morals of a Minor, and what is usually described as Violation of County Ordinance Sec. 625, subd. 1, 5, 7, & 8, PC., it was the comic blob, Blight, who arranged for Click's legal counsel. In all, a pretty penny was spent, no doubt, but in the end, Click got off with a plea of Senile Dementia and an indefinite sentence to be served not in prison but in a State Institution, where an amusing chap like Click could get the sort of attention he obviously needed.

(Blight always sent cigars at Christmas.)

The red-headed, broken-nosed whore named Wanda, seated on the edge of the eternally unmade bed, casually scanning the walls for the peekholes, rolls down her dark stockings, shows her white thighs. And nicely straightens out her hero.

"Certainly, sweetie. You just come up with an extra five dollar bill and I'll eat any damned thing in this room."

Snip-Snip-Snip. Oh yes, Blight's on the job. The ripe walls go up around him. Nicotine stained walls. Queer walls, they do exude the most subtle, edge-of-the-dream fragrance. They recall the hotel's scented past. Aromatic recollections of Bay Rum and No-Druff Hair Oil, gin, cigars, cloves and ether, rubber panties, talcum powder, lavender, and haze of toilet water, orange water, Sen-Sen. Bouquets of dime-store perfumes, eroot of Lysol, bad Bourbon: such marvelously blended flavors, evoking the damp essence of travelers long since checked out. Yet, they still linger: wistfully, the dear departed continue to return. So shy, the faint odors keep back, keep to the walls that go up forever, up past the great chandeliers, swimming in a breeze too soft to stir even the cobwebs, but the chandeliers turn with every breath, paddling through the pale, weeping light. And above the chandeliers, the light fades from gray to darkness and from gray to the ceiling. One has every right to agree with Blight. . . . Does one also have the right to disagree?

If one asks if not the ceiling, then what supports six floors of rooms? One must be patient while it is pointed out—once more, it is pointed out—that all one may be absolutely sure of is that a purported but unseen ceiling may very well support at least six flights of fancies.

One is perfectly cognizant of the implications in the preceding. One is not so incautious as to bring specific accusations into a Brief, before such accusations have been substantiated past any reasonable doubt. Yet some boxes must be built from the outside in, and some situations demand, very early, possibly before they have earned it, nonetheless they need it, the same degree of *assumption* that is accorded an invisible ceiling, and six hypothetical stories, and rooms that no one has ever entered. Officially or otherwise. All your life you may believe in rooms that you will never enter, never confirm. Then for a night, for one night only, *disbelieve*. Take this, the antithetical point of view, even though it entails a cosmography rarely encountered beyond the confines of one's forehead.

For Blight's sake, agree that he is dreaming—even though his scissors snicker, tracing outlines of lap-sized women. He is dreaming. . . . Let's say he is dreaming of many, many rooms floating over his bald head. Say that six tiers of rooms are con-

structed on that bent, massive, naked, glinting dome. . . . No
one knows *exactly* how many rooms. Not even Blight, the
nodding Nightclerk, who, in the miniscorium of his more
detailed nightmares, has furnished every one of these un-
counted rooms with the odds and ends of failure. Furnished
them in the solemn tradition of tobacco-colored highboys, dress-
ers stamped out of sheet metal, the sheets welded together,
forming four lethally sharp corners, then sprayed with chestnut and burnt-sienna paint. A superfluous number of make-
believe knotholes created with an airbrush. ("Looks damn
near like the real article," the salesmen used to say, trying to
hustle these tinny cutouts of furniture. Back in the thirties,
that was, when Detroit needed the business as badly as Grand
Rapids. . . . What would the salesmen say now, one wonders?
Years, tears, a succession of tormented travelers have chipped
the paint. And the bitterness shines through.)

Imagine those rooms at the Travelers Hotel. Imagine
them and their relation to the lobby below them. Recall that
lobby, glutted with mobs of shadows, colonies of bric-a-brac,
all multiplied in the myriad mirrors, mocked by fragrant aromas
that linger though the substance has traveled on, leaving no
forwarding address. Imagine a shrouded lobby at 1:15 A.M.
Imagine the *snip* of the Nightclerk's scissors. Voices whisper
all around him. Persons sitting still as statues, lobby specters,
behind in their rent, occupying out-of-the-way couches, hidden
behind the dusty ferns. Spider webs marry tables to chairs.
Indiscrete phantoms are encouraged to fondle themselves, and
even others, behind the broad, artificial fronds of embalmed
rubber plants.

Here in the lobby all is clutter and garble. Snippets of
paper fall around the Nightclerk's chair. Parts of heads, torso
cuttings, scraps of girls litter the floor around the roomdesk.
No wind stirs them: Here, the air hangs turgid, disturbed

only by the merest whispers, the faintest breezes, and the voracious *snip-snip* of the Nightclerk's shears.

The lobby is a world of trinkets. But the floors overhead are the *vacua horribilia*. Suspended over the lobby, over the vast accumulation of trash, are six flights of Void. Fierce *Northströms* howl down miles and miles of corridors. Windy hallways, troubled by typhoons that come tearing out of broom closets to scream down the passageways, following some secret and explicit route. These compulsive winds, winding through the deserted corridors, what are they searching for at 2:45 in the morning? Who are they chasing through the labyrinth . . . ?

Corridors giving onto more corridors. Tracking shot of hallways, stony, flaring up as the eye moves down them, following the banshee wind. These hallways: tunnels running backwards through the hotel night, veering off into more hallways, turning, twisting, tortuous channels doubling back on themselves. Intricate corridors, where inexplicable winds wander along, passing only an occasional somnambulist.

And every four and a half feet, staggered on opposite sides of each passage, a closed door. The doors are always closed in these hallways over Blight's head. And every door made of steel, painted green; and over every green door, numbers neatly stenciled in shiny black paint. At these doors, an errant wind might pause wistfully, might sigh feelingly as it wafted about the transom a moment before continuing on down the lonesome hallways.

Lonely hallways and empty rooms. For no real reason the winds raced and tore at themselves, shrieking like abandoned women, or weeping softly like lost young girls. A hundred times a night, a wind broke its heart whispering, waiting, whispering again, outside a green steel door. And rarely did anyone whisper back.

In most of the rooms, sighs went unanswered. Nothing moved, no one waited.

A tin bureau, a lumpy bed, a dripping faucet in the bathroom. A closet that will not stay shut—a warp in the wood keeps springing the door—two metal hangers, twisted around each other hang lopsided in the shallow, open closet. Sometimes a chair, a stool, a small table, sometimes not. Rooms with bath. Wafer-thin bar of gritty green soap, wrapped in paper, placed in the soap dish. One washcloth, one hand towel, one bath towel, all neatly folded over the towel bar. Tub, basin, toilet, and toilet paper; half a roll of gray, dampish toilet paper . . . toilet paper that someone has already used to wipe himself, and rerolled back, so carefully, so cunningly.

Rooms with surprises. Jokes *in absentia*. Is it really so surprising that, given the choice, the best of us go mad?

Or else, like Old Lady Blee, we live too long, take too much advantage of geriatrics, and live to see ourselves removed to rooms at the Travelers Hotel. We live alone, and not even the wind bothers to stop at our door.

So it is true, then? There are people living in those rooms over Blight's head? But anyone could see *that much*. Look how he rocks and hums to himself as he cuts. If ever a man could be called *occupied*, it was Blight.

In a hotel large as the Travelers, however, there's always room for one more. And with a Nightclerk like Blight, the more rooms he rents out, the more vacancies are charged off the dayshift.

And it was nothing but self-pity that set the wind to whining through the creatureless corridors. Of course there were *some* empty rooms, and naturally certain rooms were emptier than others. There're rooms and then there're *rooms* at a hotel like the Travelers.

There are rooms to sleep in, rooms to weep in, with the windows painted black, and old photographs pinned all over the walls. There are rooms ideally suited for rutting. The dressing-table mirror is always angled to catch the lewd ones at their passionate antics on the bed. . . .

Other rooms are built for soliloquies.

These are the rooms for the ones who come alone, drifting into the lobby with bells in their hair, no luggage. Once, twice, three times a month, they appear at the roomdesk. They need only nod and Spenser knows immediately what they want. Not a woman, not a bottle, not a bed or a bedtime story, they are past such frivolity. Past desire.

This too was the Nightclerk's duty. Accommodations for these silent travelers, frightful holy men on their way to heaven. They pause at the desk to pick up their roomkeys. Pay in advance: they have their money in their hands, at the ready. Then, their fountain pens filled with cold blood, they sign their enemy's names on the register. And though the Nightclerk may wish them goodnight, they answer never. Once in a very long while, one may smile. But that's all. A little, cracked smile. (The Nightclerk saved every single one that he got: there weren't very many, but they filled a cigar box.)

The Nightclerk would watch as they walked to the elevator. He would remain standing until the elevator doors closed.

Sometimes they didn't come down for a fortnight—the hotel's maid service was hardly regular. But sooner or later everybody got found, and carried out in a canvas bag, *Prop. City Morgue.*

Whether they made themselves dead in bed by sleeping pills, jumped out the window, or slit their throats and bloodied the bathroom floor; whether they twisted a pillowcase into a noose and hung themselves up in the shallow closet (and *that's* the real reason why the door won't close); whether they got dead by morning, or sooner, or later, eventually all the suicides turn up.

And housemaids at the Travelers would develop the curious facility of being able to divine, just from the way a green door looked—green like all the other doors, but *different*—when she wheeled her laundry cart up to it, even the dullest maid soon learned to tell whether or not a corpse lay stiffening behind it.

No blame on Blight.

He rents rooms, he tries to please everyone. He listens to the hard-luck stories, and he is often listed on the morbidity report, Form ACD 222, line D, after the words

DECEASED LAST SEEN ALIVE BY————————————.

And that too is the Nightclerk's duty. It isn't all snuff and fancy magazines. He wishes no man harm, yet he must issue the ultimate rejection. If not he, then who would sort the morning mail just before going off the nightshift? Who would sort the mail? Who would censor it? Who would have to make the final decision, which in certain extremely unfortunate circumstances demanded the supreme penalty to be rubber-stamped onto the envelope:

NO SUCH PERSON KNOWN AT THIS ADDRESS

and

Refused, Return to Sender, fare-thee-well.

In what way is Blight responsible for this, for any of this? Why should a clerk be intimidated, whispered at, be magicked from twilight to sunrise for situations created by Authority? Certainly no one supposed that Blight was more than a six hundred and seventeen pound Nightclerk?

Why should anyone think that he had something to do with putting just-maimed kittens in the airshaft, to scream half the night, to drive the old ladies, Mrs. Blee, Mrs. Flee, and Mrs. Kupperman-North, to weep with the bedclothes wrapped over their ears? And even when the kittens were finally disposed of, by two huge firemen in great ugly boots, the old women continued to hear the kittens crying, even though it wasn't possible. . . .

. . . even though it wasn't possible. Even though he had more than enough to dream about, with six floors of doors for rent, and enough beds for nearly every bug.

No matter what lies are whispered, let it be clearly and definitively stated, for the benefit of those who affect ignorance of the True Facts in this matter: a Nightclerk does not go out of his way to interfere with, hinder, or in any manner disturb the guests.

He doesn't have to.

Nobody sleeps at the Travelers. . . . Not when there's a Stag Party going on. No one has yet explained why a Nightclerk should go banging around in a dirty old airshaft when he can lounge comfortably around the lobby, reading novels, dipping snuff, scissoring magazines, offering convention suites at special rates.

After all, it only takes a pimp, a few whores, some dirty movies, and a bunch of good guys, and what the hell, it's Zoo Night at the Travelers Hotel!

And not even a kilo of Blight's miraculous snuff would have permitted an old lady's wrinkled soul to sneak off to sleep, on those gala nights when they open the cages and the hippos are turned loose to race up and down the windy corridors, and the apes of Yappii are set to howling and pounding the walls. When they put the lustful donkeys in with the rutting goats, whinnying and pawing the worn carpets, then, what chance was there for sleep?

Sleep on Stag Nite?

No. Not even if you were deaf . . . for the Boys raised such hell that the whole structure shook, trembled under their hooves. And the pounding on the wall next door, getting louder and louder.

If you can't hear it, still you can feel it.

It's that crazy gang of stags up on the fourth floor.

The fourth . . .? Then what the hell are they doing up there on the *sixth?* Who are they throwing off the roof? Of course one could be mistaken. At night, the eyes play funny tricks. All kinds of gags, Ha-Ha, screams.

But nobody ever *really* gets hurt; not very badly, that is, not when the Boys get together, after business hours, they never throw anyone off the roof, and so what if they relax a little and maybe once in a while throw a little party named Joycie or Judy or something like that into a bathtub full of half-melted ice cubes? That's a far cry from throwing her out the window, or off the roof. The newspapers always exaggerate these things.

It's true that one of the fellows probably did take a touch too much and got sick and threw up in the elevator. And that's a nuisance, but not murder. The porter will clean it up, just as soon as he finishes sweeping up the glass on the fourth. . . .

A couple of windows are bound to be broken, along with a number of drinks spilt, cigarette holes burnt into the bedspreads and mattresses, numbers tattooed on the chambermaid's forearm. Business is business, and competitors are regularly drugged and locked up in hallway linen closets. . . . The dayshift always finds them and releases them in plenty of time to get to the office. And whatever damage has been done to hotel property need only be itemized and billed to the Boys. It's their party . . . it's their night to howl. . . .

. . . And look who they woke up!

Three dead gangsters; padded shoulders, pinstripe suits;

narrow, cruel, pockmarked Sicilian faces. Their throats neatly
cut above their celluloid collars, bullet holes in their backs, and
their eyes smoking in their skulls, this trio had wangled a pre-
ternatural writ of *habeas corpus,* and has stepped out of the
wallpaper to be with us tonight. (Applause)

Thankyou. On behalf of three old-timers, three deceased
veterans of a thousand such stag nights. . . .

    1st Gangster: Bring on the broads!

    2nd Gangster: Call *this* a stag party?

    3rd Gangster: We climbed out of our coffins for this?
                This ain't no stag party . . . this is a
                fag party. . . !

. . . and even the doorknobs fell off laughing. *This ain't no stag
party . . . this is a fag party!* Get it? All the Boys wink at each
other; give each other the suggestive elbow, the nudge. Get it?
What the hell, it's a party. What the hell, all the Boys are in
the same business. Buying and selling. Putting out hot numbers: this season's big seller, a combination fur-lined pocket and
artificial finger. The Boys, manufacturers of comprehensive
lines of gadgets, instruments, devices to humiliate the female. . . .

    It's a fag party!

The five-room suite rang with nasty laffs. The plaster on
the ceiling got the gag and cracked maliciously. In one of the
rooms, the portable movie screen was still up . . . tobacco smoke
thick in all the rooms, making a mystery of salesmanagers, pot-
bellies, initialed belt-buckles, jowls ghastly. Aggressive. . . .
Twenty-five hundred Boys (one source reported) stood around
the Peach Blossom Suite, drinking whiskey, holding hands,
listening to three dead and dirty old men, three dead dogs, three
mad dogs barking for broads. The Boys applauded and waved
their handkerchiefs.

They began to drift out of the room where the speeches
were still going on. Half the floor had been reserved for the

convention. The Boys went wandering, looking for girls to do.

Crew cuts and bald heads, hotshots, cold cuts; cigar butts floating in the toilet. Who set fire to the wastebasket? Who pissed out the window? Who called the name of old Mister Galapus, the crapulous occupant of room 609?

Who called his name so sweetly. . . ? Who made the old man come awake with an awful jolt, sitting bolt upright in his bed, spitting blood into his hand, his weak, frightened old eyes searching the room for the voice that had called him. . . ?

"This is Galapus, damnit," he coughed and he snorted. "It's Galapus! Who's calling me . . . ? Who wants me . . . ? Who . . . ?"

". . . wants to kiss it before I break it?" bawled Vaseline Sally, Queen of the Stags, doing her act while the Boys sat around in their underwear, belching and admiring each other's horns.

In addition to Sally, scattered throughout the suite, the troop of party gals, Niki, Viki, Tricky, and Jane did dances and sang songs that brought a tear to many a manly eye.

This was no fag party, this was a stag party! And a night the Boys would not soon forget. A night of rousing good fellowship, of pretty girls and strong whiskey and dirty movies and crazy things done by strangers, by travelers trapped overnite in hotel rooms. . . .

In short, this was the Night that the Kreature called Kandy got hers.

II

THE TRAVELERS HOTEL
in the heart of downtown Frisco .

claimed the letterheads of the few flyspecked sheets of paper
that remained, souvenir of the days when the Travelers still
bothered with the niceties of stationery.

Quaint thought. Perhaps in those once upon a time days,
downtown Frisco actually had a heart. A little too quaint . . .
more likely it was just an old-fashioned way of selling hotel
space: Sales pitches have changed since then, changed just like
the salesmen themselves. The fickle Commercial Traveler,
once the bread and butter of this hotel, now goes elsewhere to
get eaten. He's traveled on to the plastic, Buck Rogers motels,
there to have his credit cards honored, his baths thermoheated;
to sleep on foam, under foam, in comforting proximity to his
automobile.

The traveling men are gone from the blighted downtown,
and undoubtedly they took the heart along with them. They
took the heart and left a few little trinkets, like the last fifty-six
sheets of the hotel stationery, hidden so long that they've been
forgotten, locked up in a drawer that used to have a key, in a
broken-down desk that nobody ever sits at, in the back of a
rarely used office in this hotel. A hotel too large to be lost, too
ugly to forget. An uncomfortable landmark in the heartless
downtown.

A downtown and a hotel that had both seen better days.
Better nights. . . .

The nights now seem so strange: not wicked as they once
were, no longer sporty, not gay, not reckless and dashing. Only
. . . uneasy. A miniature moral played out by amateurs on every
street corner, and the handwriting on every wall. Of Signes and
Portents there is no lack, and even the wind whispers of a beast

risen, of the holocaust that approaches. The wind of alarm, crossing the city with its tattered herald, yesterday's newspaper blowing noisily down the lonesome avenues of night, blowing from streetlamp to cockeyed streetlamp.

Down in nitetown. A patrol car is always coming around the corner, creeping slowly up the block, curbside; cop window rolled down, leather arm bent, poking through the open window, .38 caliber cop's eyes search the faces of the sidewalk stragglers. Looking for whom? Only the Mayor and the Father of Police know who is tagged *it* for tonight. The squad cars get their orders, follow directions, full descriptions of persons wanted, typed and clipped to a clipboard. Nobody knows why.

At certain hours in the night, when hardly anyone is looking, the Travelers Hotel, that gargantuan, gloomy, superannuated structure, firetrap, a vertical cemetery where the travelers' hearts are buried, hotel where the Nightclerk clerks, detaches itself from its concrete foundation and rises: silent as a sea-bat, the enormous menace glides, all grace and soundless, through the noisy, deep, queer, and very dangerous currents of night. This is the haunted building that feeds in the deceitful downtown waters, among the uncharted shoals and the shifting reefs that run just below the level of consciousness from the wine-soaked panhandle of Mission Street (street of missions long ago abandoned, now wandering without visible means of support or purpose up and down the friendless sidewalks) and on to Market Street, that avenue of streetlamps and steel shutters, dummies in the windows of department stores, unplugged for the night. Then cross Market and thence into the bright, garish, brassy, violently troubled waters of the Tenderloin.

On these obscene streetlets, the seachange is most evident, and most voracious. Here bloom the poison grottoes, the stripclubs, whorebars, and the depraved arcades; other haunts of public, puerile, ha'penny pleasures. Here the stale cafeterias where feed the queerfish, the great spotted suckers and the transparent blowfish, the besotted flounder. Here the fatty-fishes come to wait for friends, while persons trim and murderous as tigersharks also wait. Cafeteria creatures all.

And in and out of the Greyhound cafe, Fester's cafeteria, Belli's Good All-Nite Eats, other interesting, late hour dining spots downtown, drift streetwalking depravities. Bait for the visiting firemen and other trout that must be caught with a tickle. . . .

And down at the end of every street, like the downtown moon, the Travelers Hotel stands overhead. That insatiable body rises and falls with the midnight tide, ingesting without discrimination whatever, whoever, floats through its revolving doors and into the shadowy maw, the lobby where the Nightclerk bobs and nods in squidlike dreams of rich nightfulls. Great solitary, nocturnal swallowings.

He yawned furiously. Old habit. He wasn't sleepy, not in the slightest. Not in the least. He was the Nightclerk; catnaps aside, he had not slept for nearly nine years. Of course, his was a very special case.

Even so, everyone, even the special ones, must expect to yawn now and then. No one's life is entirely free of monotony.

remained as he had left her, on her hands and knees. She no longer wondered who would be next. Since she understood now that she had no choice but to remain until all were satisfied, the question was merely academic.
THE END

It was 12:31 in the morning. He closed the book, *Ordeal of Lady K.*, and dropped it into a drawer on the left-hand side of the roomdesk. From a drawer on the right-hand side, Blight extracted a long, gleaming pair of scissors, and a magazine full of pictures. Pretty pictures.

He spread the magazine open on his lap, then, scissors in hand, bent to his work while the vast, empty lobby slobbered around him.

✄

Of course, her Real Name wasn't Kandy. That was just what they called her, when they called her. Which was less and less as time went by. For all her names, the fact remained, she was too old to be working these stags. A case of Kandy tasted too often. . . . Now look at her, skunk drunk and naked as a jaybird, squatting on top of a six-foot high chiffonier, and a roomful of Boys, giggling softly while she raves. She'll fly like a swan from bureau to bed, eight feet from her perch.

"Ten dollars to your twelve, she doesn't clear the headboard," wagers a wag in his gold and sky-blue undershorts. The Boys never take off their shoes: black shoes and black rayon stockings held up by unsmiling garters.

"Fly like a what . . . ?"

"Like a swan, you swine!" Kandy unsteadily rose to her feet atop the highboy. The top of her dark head brushed the ceiling. The room stretched below her: the bed, a target ringed by her fans, the Boys, who whistled and clapped their hands. . . .

"Kandy, come down!"

But before she does, a descriptive sentence or two would not be out of order.

As she sways, looming large from the dresser top, she is a woman turning to lard. Her breasts are enormous, but flabby and deflated, hanging halfway down her belly. From shoulders to ankles she is covered with scars, some quite curious. And she wouldn't explain them . . . though any fool in the room was welcome to her beat-up backside, her scars were her own. And nobody yet had guessed her secret. Nobody suspected . . . nobody could imagine who she used to be. Way back when. The days before she had been licked down to this trade name Kandy: stag party goo, artificial coloring, corn starch, dry powdered fats skin and.

(The discursive *and*.)

And if the Nightclerk had not looked after her, if he had not made her employment a condition of the reduced rate he offered the convention's pimp, then who would have employed this old, whipped whore at any but scrub-hag's chores? If not for the Nightclerk, who would have had her, though once upon a time she might very well have been a most delectable, toothsome Kandy, she was now a fat and flaccid Kandy. Rancid, after a fashion of speaking. To put it bluntly, the slut would have starved, had not Blight looked after her.

She hated him.

She said he had magicked her and was continuing to do so.

This wasn't true. He was sorry for what had happened and only wanted to make amends. He was sorry that the only work he could find her was over his head at the roistering party, where they jeered at her, and pelted her with breadcrumbs and olives. If she didn't like it, she could always get dressed and get her a mop and pail. . . . If she didn't like it, she didn't have to let them tease her into a back room, up on a dresser . . . what the hell was she doing?

How could this degraded, naked, shameless, drunken, depraved creature, this ungrateful, unlovely, unnatural female be, not only the Mistress of the Nightclerk, but the most Important Woman of her Age, as well?

Though many hounds had spat between her legs, had any gotten inside her?

The stags come and go, shedding their antlers after the party. Virile today, tomorrow in the Bay; that's a stag's life.

They are brutes, and know not when they are in the company of a Saint.

Kandy blows kisses down to the crowd. Seven men with hairy legs, gathered around an iron bedstead. Waiting.

(Could Blight have foreseen this?)

She spreads her arms out wide, embracing them all. And

naked,

she flew.........

.........Swiveling like a turret gunner, Blight spun on the ball bearings of his plush chair, and wheeled over to the switchboard. The girlie magazine spread across his lap, he exchanged the scissors for a headset, and plugged himself in.

"Desk," he said mildly and glanced down at the magazine.

MARRIED MEN   GET MUTUAL SATISFACTION

A quivering falsetto pinked his ear. "Hello, is this the Desk? Hello, Operator, would you connect me with the Room-desk, please."

"Desk," purred Blight, who couldn't be ruffled by voices on the telephone. "Yes sir, this is the Desk, sir. How may we serve you?"

"Oh . . . well, I don't need anything. I mean, the reason I called down is because I have to report a pervert in room . . ."

"Just a minute, what do you mean, *you have to*? Nobody *has to* report perverts; people do it because they like to."

"Now you look here, Mister Whoever you are down there," the voice began to wind up, but Blight cut in.

"About this pervert, is it one of our guests, or one of yours?"

"One of mine . . . !"

GETTING ENOUGH of what every man craves?

French Powders
show you how

Blight's eye scanned the page. He said nothing for a few heart-beats, time enough to let the voice hear him breathe heavily into the receiver. Then Blight whispered, "What's the Pervert doing, hey?"

From the evil titter that Blight got back, he knew that he had guessed the right voice. "Are they having a party?" teased Blight. "Tell me, what kind of party . . . ?"

"Ah, Captain . . ." sighed the voice, near to tears, "listen, I'll tell you what he's doing, this pervert . . . whisperwhisper-shhhwhispershhh." O what a vile voice! What an insinuating voice! What a won't-you-please-speak-louder voice.

"Tsk-tsk," trumped Blight, and taking the bull by the horns he turned him upside-down, and demanded to know, unequivocally.

"I demand to know," Blight refused to equivocate. "Are they licking the wineinsap?"

"We must have a bad connection."

But Blight poured on. Now chafing, now mocking, now sympathetic. "How awful it must be for you, seeing a Pervert do *that* and then having a bad connection on top of everything else. Just dreadful . . ."

"Say," the voice was slow, but not impossible. It was beginning to have a few doubts. "Say, is this the Roomdesk? Am I speaking to the Roomdesk down in the lobby?"

"No sir. This is the mezzanine. They've given you the Nightdesk. Just a jiffy, sir, and I'll flash the operator . . ." Blight's fingers flew. Flick-flick. "Operator, give this call to Roomdesk, extension 999," Blight said to himself, plugging the voice into hole 999.

LINGER CREAM

Blight rang again. And turned the page.

Down in sub-basement C, a wall-phone trilled self-consciously. It was the first time in years that anyone had rung extension 999, and even the motes of dust falling slantwise in the haze shimmering around the incinerator paused, astonished. Then the telephone rang again, triumphantly, confirming itself; and dust fell no more, but danced with excitement, for somewhere it is written that if the phone rings twice. . . .

. . . a hand with only three fingers reached out of the cement gloom of sub-basement C, and stealthily, furtively, picked up the receiver, cautious as a shoplifter.

"Hello!" buzzed the voice. "Hello, is this the Desk? Hello, I'm calling to report a Pervert . . ."

". . . . . . . Blight?"

"Here," said the Nightclerk, back at the switchboard. Give one voice a thrill and every voice in the city wants at you. ". . . do something for you?" the Nightclerk muttered. It was one of those nights.

And it was worse, far worse then he had imagined.

"She's dead, Blight. She died like an eagle."

"How's that? Who's this calling?" The lobby around him smelt the blood. Shadows pressed closer, trying to hear. "Who is dead?"

"Eagle, swan, what's the difference?" the telephone muttered. "She died like a dog, and that's all that counts. I thought you'd like to be the first to know."

"Ow," said Blight slowly, beginning to understand. "So it's like that, is it?"

"I'm sorry. Yes, that's it."

"Can you tell me how it happened?"

"Certainly. She didn't clear the headboard," the caller said shortly and clicked off.

Blight sat at the board and minutes went by. He fumbled for his snuffbox, found it, then dropped it. He made no move to pick it up. The magazine on his lap, he shoved it off. It was finished. 3:29 A.M. In the right-hand drawer of the roomdesk, an unread novel waits.

THE SLAVE SET,

but first, the Nightclerk must do his duty, must dial that old familiar number. . . .

"General Hospital, Emergency Desk. Grabow speaking."

"This is Blight, I'm calling from the Travelers Hotel, downtown. I'm calling to report an accident . . ."

". . . I did it because she was cherry," growled Big Joe, not troubling to zip up his pants. "Sure I did, and so would you if you had the nerve, or in plain English, the balls . . ."

"How well did you know her?" Lieutenant Dearie stood over Blight. The ambulance had hauled her away; Blight had already filled out the Jane Doe. But still the Lieutenant must stand over Blight, must speak to him in a loud, ugly voice. "Come on, Blight. Put that book down, I want some answers. The woman, who was she? Where was she from? Come on, Blight, the story. You know it. Spill it!" The lieutenant was big shouldered, tight lipped; he looked like a crook, and he was a bully.

Blight ignored him, tried to go on reading.

"Stop it," screamed Bubbles, "because I can't stand it anymore! I beg you, stop!"

"Who was she, Blight? Answer me, or . . ."

Blight lowered his book. "Get away from me, Dearie," he said very simply. "Everyone has secrets. I have mine, and,

Dearie, *you have yours.*" The menace in those last three words made the short hairs rise on the Lieutenant's neck. The Nightclerk smiled as the cop's hand twitched towards his pistol.

"Go find you a citizen to shoot, Lieutenant," Blight was saying, in a tone that made the policeman look over his shoulder. "Go someplace else, Dearie. Bother somebody else. But leave us nightclerks alone. We know about you, Dearie, so leave us alone. We know about you and the children and..."

"Alright, Blight." The Lieutenant put away his notebook.

"... and naturally these things aren't trusted to memory," Blight droned on. "Records carefully drawn, sworn, attested, sealed, signed, notarized, everything legal in my lawyer's safe, and my instructions in case of death or prolonged absence, these records to be delivered to the Attorney General. A photostatic copy to be delivered to the Mayor's office. Another copy to the..."

"Yes, Spenser, yes..." Lieutenant Dearie backed away. "Please, Spenser, don't tell. Don't tell on me..."

"GO!" thundered the Nightclerk. And the Lieutenant ran.

Now Blight is alone. Six hundred and eighteen pounds of blubber, why is he weeping? The swivel chair rocks like an overcrowded lifeboat, bobbing in the sorrowful sea. *She is dead. She is gone.* His bald dome nods, his famous yellow eyes stare through a wash of tears.

Alone in the lobby. 4:08 A.M. No one beats a muffled drum, slowly, lowly; an echo of a drum, more exactly. Faintly, faintly. Far away and long, long ago.

Now the hydra-headed mist comes seeping into the ghastly lobby. It curls around the shipwrecked furniture, the broken hulks, the sinister forms, shifting imperceptibly on the ocean floor. A ghostyard of shadows, and shapes too familiar ... suspicious and uncomfortably intimate voices call him out by his first name. . . .

"Spenser," they call. "James Spenser Blight."

Collapsed in his custom-built swivel chair, the corpulent shepherd of the downtown niteflocks, keeper of one secret too many, now turned his palms up, signifying that he was ready to tell the whole truth.

Men have been locked away for much less.

"Don't tell! Please don't tell!" the shadows come running from every part of the Travelers Hotel. They wring their hands and beseech so piteously.

"Don't tell! Sweet Blight, don't tell . . . !" they cry like the wind in the sky, like floorboards in agony, like the rustle of petticoats in the hushed lobby. Indeed it is wonderful to hear an entire hotel begin squeaking in terror. Only let a Nightclerk threaten to tell what he knows. . . . He could bring the roof down on all of our heads!

Fear. Totally unrealistic, based on atavistic prejudices. Nightclerks are chosen for their humanitarian virtues, why will people persist in believing they do ill?

Why should Spenser make trouble for ghosts? Nothing was further from his intention.

"This morning, at approximately 3:00 A.M., a 42-year-old witch died as a result of multiple contusions. According to reliable sources, the woman's head injuries were received in the course of a wild game of charades, when the unfortunate lady attempted to imitate a duck. The accident took place in a downtown hotel. Names are being withheld until the next-of-kin have been notified . . ." Blight cleared his throat. He looked around the empty lobby.

"She is gone," he whispered in a soft, wondering voice. Then, in a louder voice, he went on reading the Official Statement.

"Although positive identification will never be made, authorities are reasonably certain that this woman was the most wonderful female of her generation. Suffice it to say that her name is a household term. . . . We all knew her. We loved her. She is gone."

(Dark horses move through the muffled, predawn streets carrying the early editions. All over the city, the women of the streets, under the drowning streetlamps waiting, are whispering the bad news to each other. Flags will be flown upside down for a fortnight. On the Embarcadero, they are firing cannons into the Bay. Workmen have already begun repainting Golden Gate Bridge in black and funereal grays. Now it is starting, the dismal rain that falls slantwise across the unmarked grave. The keening and wailing of the inconsolable mourners. Soon the suicides and the immolations will commence. They will call out her name as they step off the edge. Only wait until they understand the extent of their loss, then you will hear how a people can weep.)

"This woman," Blight droned on through the list of honors: "Saint-in-her-lifetime, and Perpetual Martyr. Imitated by movie actresses all over the world; playwrights and poets have plagiarized her adventures. Toy manufacturers have made dolls in her likeness. Her masks have become so well known that it was necessary for her to go about unmasked. She was the inventor and lifelong patroness of Sundays For Dead Children, and this earned her the blessing and prayers of millions of parents whose offspring had passed beyond. Thanks to That Lady, one Sunday a year was set aside . . . and the public parks were all crowded with mothers and fathers out walking with their dead children.

"Yet her own parents had not spoken to her since her twenty-first birthday.

"She was a marvel of contradictions. Born rich, she died a pauper. Her star was glorious. She lived like a Goddess, and she died like a drab, naked and drunk in a room full of lechers. She was taken away like a sack full of garbage, to lie in the morgue, tagged like a hunk of cold baggage, stretched out among strangers. But her heavenly body, without any doubt, lies in state; in some August Hall of Queens, she takes her eternal rest, attended by her royal sisters, Jeanne d'Arc, Nefertiti, Justine, Sappho, Madame Curie.

"She was a bizarre and exotic beauty. . . !" Blight's voice rose dangerously. The lobby drew back, away from his wrath.

"And long shall we languish till another of her measure shall come again!" He lamented with the tongues of a hundred rabbis. "She shall not soon come again!"

And a sober voice answered, "Amen."

Blight rubbed his eyes. "She was my finest creation," he said very softly. "She was my masterpiece."

It was true. Perfectly true. Or rather, *it was the beginning of truth.*

III

Now shall dreadful things be told, bitter things to make one weep, res amara flebilis, res quidem, coqitatu terribilis. Bitter things to make one weep, horrible to think, terrible to think. Insipiencia junentorum stupenda bestialitate transcendens, which surpass the limits of debauchery. . . .

Spenser was reading this forbidding introduction, penned in Katy's spider-web hand, written diagonally across a page in her journal, dated two months previous, or, to be exact, three days after their wedding.

At the moment, they were on a steamship, somewhere in the North Atlantic. Katy was sitting on the bed, painting her toenails. Their stateroom was very large and painted white, with gold trim and gold accoutrements; and the sea ran high past their portholes.

"What dreadful things?" Spenser sprawled on the chaise longue. "We haven't had time to surpass the limits of anything, yet."

"It wasn't a statement," she answered, not looking up from her toes. "It wasn't a statement, it was a prophecy . . . Oh Goddamn!" The stateroom swung from under them and the nail polish splashed on the floor.

Spenser stopped reading. Typically, she had begun her journal in the middle of one of his notebooks. "You're convinced that you're a witch, aren't you?" he accused her.

"No, not yet," she accused him right back. "But you did promise that you'd make me one, didn't you? Or have you forgotten?"

Katy was a rich girl, born to it. She had turned twenty-one only a few weeks ago, and she was a great beauty. No wonder then she was so sure of herself. She wished for mantic gifts, and since she wanted them, she did not for an instant doubt that they would be given. A spoiled and well-sheltered brat tossing her curls and demanding the moon...?

That wasn't Katy. Her story was different. All of her stories...

She had been in and out of mental institutions since she was twelve, and a registered sex offender since her fifteenth birthday. It had all been very interesting but nothing that she'd seen at Juvenile Hall, or later, in prison; no treatment applied in private sanatoriums and public lunatoriums, and the occasional experimental station that got to try her once or twice; nothing here and nothing there. Nothing in the *curriculum vitre et propre,* featured in the prospectus of the expensive finishing schools where she'd stop off for a semester or two, gather academic honors and promptly get popped into the next madhouse; nothing in either sermon or court sentence, no medical diagnosis, no house mother's well-meant counsel; in short, nothing encountered awake or asleep could keep Katy from her periodic investigationals. And as for her fantastic notions, those unreasonable convictions, & etcetera, they did not grow less fantastic, more reasonable, as she grew older and lovelier. On the contrary, those punishable opinions found much to substantiate themselves. And her guesses were too accurate, too often.

Fully a quarter of a millennium ahead of her contemporaries, Katy had submitted early to the Visionary's castigation. She had endured electrotherapy, sadistic matrons, arch headmistresses, and a privileged but not altogether enviable family life that was climaxed and culminated with the seduction of her brother when she was nineteen and he a fresh-faced prep-school lad of sixteen summers... this peccadillo was discovered almost before it happened, and subsequently—she was later told—her brother was sterilized by surgeons in her father's employ. The old man was intractable on certain farfetched points. But there wasn't much more he could do to Katy except ship her back to the Bad Place. Back to the matrons, the *treatments,* and the solitude that's granted only to crazy dolls and very, very clever women, when they desperately need a place to hide.

And that was just where Spenser found her, better than a year after the incest fiasco; stashed in a private room, well off the wards and away from all but the most determined visitors.

Blight was eminently qualified for inclusion in this category. It was, after all, Blight, before anyone else, who discerned in Katy that rare spirit, *lusus naturae,* a freak of nature. And this he perceived in the single opportunity, the four seconds that Providence vouchsafed him one forenoon. . . . When they were wheeling an unconscious Katy from the Treatment Room to her own cell. It was against the law to take her through the halls during the hours when patients and staff might possibly be loitering about, but a new nurse had been assigned to Katy, a nurse not yet familiar with the rules.

And there was Blight, in fortune's lap, idly leafing through a magazine, just in case someone was watching. There was Blight so casual in the night nurse's cubbyhole. The door was open; he was careful to stand in full sight of the hall, flipping the pages of *Truest Detective.* No harm in that. While a wax impression hardened in the keyhole of the Night Nurse's medicine cabinet. Hi-Ho, that was Blight killing time. Blight standing in the lucky spot, he just happened to look up as a young woman, strapped to a gurney, rolled by.

It took him a week to discover who she was. It took three weeks more to win her threshold. But from there it was only fifteen minutes till they were engaged in that amoric activity that Katy referred to as *passing the ghost.*

Blight's snap sight had hit the mark where it felt best. She was indeed that woman. He confirmed it in the first, hurried half-hour when, with her door locked from the inside, the orderly properly paid off and posted, Katy and Blight were ritualing together.

After he'd had her, he knew he must save her. Must away with her though iron doors are locked at night, though bloodhounds and the State Police, hospital thugs, searchlights sweeping the hospital grounds, the barbed wire hidden in the high, well-clipped hedges, this and more, the ten thousand precision-ground parts of the Invincible Capture Machine, were set to grind against them, still Blight was not overawed. There was a will, there was a way.

And while it may be perfectly true to say that in those years, the sword was never very far from Blight's hand, still, the same may be said of so many young men. At one time or another, who has not put his hand in a murder? Which is not to admit guilt or connection with the brutal slaying of two psychiatric nurses, a medical typist who didn't deserve it, and a technician, a hydrotherapist who had no business getting between a psychotic and the last iron door. That such a horrendous affair should occur on the night of Blight's and Katy's departure is entirely circumstantial, and no one to date has succeeded in proving otherwise. For, not to beg the point nor split a hair, it must be recalled that in addition to Blight and Katy, eleven patients from the R (Restricted, i.e., violent) Ward took advantage of the temporary breakdown in institutional security, the confusion and the blinding terror occasioned by the four-fold homicide.

So then, why Blight and not one of the eleven rippers from R Ward?

Should any fingers be pointed when almost none of the facts are known?

These are the insidious forms of accusations that must infuriate the mildest among us.

However, this is not the place to essay the above incident in its full and deserving detail. A time will come. Till then, suffice to say, Blight and his lady got out from the clutches of that grubby asylum, and, by dint of their courage, their intelligence, and the excellent offices of a highly placed and extremely Confidential Clerk, at the Bureau of Records, Files & Hospital Secrets, all traces of their names were removed from every document, application, memo, index, etc., etc., that could associate them with the institution where the aforementioned murders did occur. Quite a labor, this *entire erasure*, extending to special diets, laundry lists, visitor cards, bed charts, memoranda. Even a med student's term paper on Blight's bowel movements was traced and destroyed. These removals continued through the myriad cross-references, double files, and triple-checks found in bound stacks at the Technical Archives. But which may be found there no more; there, or anywhere else, save this MS. Not even the Chief of Clerks, himself, could have found official evidence of Blight's or Katy's past, so thoroughly had the confidentially employed Clerk done his work. Not even the Senior Clerk-in-Charge could have found any record of Blight and Katy, not even if he had looked himself. And of course there wasn't any reason in the world why he should do that.

Then Blight went to deal with Katy's malevolent father. This *pater ogre* was something less than formidable: hardly magick at all. Just an ignorant old Evil, who for all his windy boasts and vicious threats was unable to discover one antidote among the many, many charms, serums, counterspells and home remedies—most of them described in any halfway competent toxicopoeia—to preserve him from that old wives' tale,

la fattura della morte: a primitive Sicilian enchantment wherein a lemon is used to kill a man.

In just such an anticlimactic fashion are the petty monsters done away with when they demonstrate their ambitious
stupidity, when they overstep their poison and dare look dirty
at Blight.

But where is the glory in insect squashing? Was Blight
just another hero tearing the wings off flies? One more great
wizard, torturing caterpillars and cockroaches with a lit cigarette?

We know better.

Merciful, when mercy was least expected, Spenser had
the old dog dragged off to a *home* that specialized in the care
and confinement of uncooperative elders. Not that the old boy
was entirely uncooperative. It took a pinch here, a twist there,
but soon enough Blight had the necessary signatures, the
thumb print, the key to the safe deposit box. Clickety-click.
Katy and a modest fortune passed from Daddy's hands to
Blight's. Why should Spenser wish the oldster further harm?
And an agreement is an agreement, but it was only with the
greatest difficulty that Blight managed to spare Papa's life, for
Katy did clamor for his heart, his liver, his snake, and Blight
was hard put to convince her that she need not gobble. The
old man should be left intact, Blight appeased her, pointing
out that this way, whenever she had the yen to settle old in-
justices, she could do so, and do so again and again.

Blight championed the proposition that satisfaction is
sweetest and revenge most palatable when partaken of a nibble
at a time.

Thus having appeased convention, honored their contracts, and removed their fingerprints, they took the money
out of the deposit box and traveled to New York City, New
York, where, after some months of delay, they finally obtained

passports, marriage certificate, various writs, and certain gratifications of an anomalous nature.

Katy's fancies, it may be remarked here, were not only queer, they were extraordinarily complicated. There were occasions when Blight, major stylist though he was, found himself hard-pressed to facilitate his leggy, dark-haired, succubus-eyed bride. Why lie? Why dissemble? Blight more than once had his back to the wall, and what choice but to face the challenge, to call each demon by his or her given name and number? So he did. And by so doing made his way through Katy's disordered senses.

Put it this way. Say that Blight's interests were best served by the maintenance and operational explorations down that fey passage, and say that in the course of those expeditions he found it necessary to commit those acts of sabotage, so-called, which materially contribute to the continued state of giddy disorder, the criminal derangement of the organs of perception. Or, more explicitly, Blight will receive credit for the tampering, the tinkering, the rearranging of those lights and shadows that flicker on the periphery of the higher centers of intelligence. Watch how it's done. The deft twist to the phrase mumbled in a dream, overheard by one like Blight, turns fantasy to fact, has the power to strengthen any delusion, will give substance to mere notions, does add the authentic detail to the broad, rough sketch.

For example, let Katy come rushing, flushed and breathless, into the bedroom of their hotel suite on an afternoon not long after their marriage. Say that Spenser has been napping on the circular bed, and that Katy has been out shopping, strolling through the park, visiting construction sites, wherever it is that she goes when she goes out. Then let her come back, bursting into the bedroom with a touch of fever in her eyes, with her hair uncombed, and her blouse—he sees when she lets her coat slide from her shoulders—her blouse torn in two places.

"Spenser! O wake up, Spenser!"

"Ummm, yes, yes," Blight intoned, waking behind his voice. "Yes, my dear, and whom have you been getting away from?"

"Please, Spenser, please listen to me. . . !" Katy's face, colored one instant by the ruddy tint of flight, could in the next instant pale to reflect the *extremis* of terror. Tricky as a chameleon she was; but this should not be interpreted as an indication that she was an alarmist, an untruthful woman, a fabricator, or a purveyor of hysterical and extravagant fictions. To be perfectly honest, Katy had in common with most of her sex that inability to see much further than the Truth, even when that truth was a complete sham. An exceptional woman in numerous respects, she had the most mediocre imagination, and almost no talent for making up dreams. Such a literal Katy. What she dreamt, actually happened. Sometimes before she dreamt it, sometimes afterwards. What matter? The time-sequence is less consistent and more arbitrary than the weather. Did it happen on Wednesday or on Thursday? In the month of May, or in the Ember Days of Lent? Clerks will not fail to appreciate the insignificance of these details.

"Spenser! Don't you understand . . . a man with no head chased me through the park!" Katy was still panting from her flight. She barely choked the story out. "He was waiting for me at the bridge behind the zoo. He was waiting for me . . . I got away . . . through the bushes. . . !"

Blight glanced at her legs. Yes, her stockings were in shreds.

"Spenser, I'm afraid!"

"Yes of course . . ." Blight yawned elaborately. Deceptively. "Eh, did he hurt you, this *homme sans tête?*"

"I ran," she heaved.

"Yes, you ran. But . . ."

"And he chased me! He ran after me!"

"I understand. He was trying to catch you. But you don't know for a fact that he meant to harm you, now do you?"

"Spenser, are you out of your mind?" Katy gave him the strangest look. "Did you hear me. . . ? I said, a *man with no head* . . ." She broke off. She heard the toilet flush.

"Who's here? Aren't we alone?"

"No dear, we're not alone. Not exactly."

Katy closed her eyes. She heard the water splashing in the wash basin.

". . . a very old friend of mine," Spenser was saying as the bathroom door opened. Somebody came into the bedroom. Katy kept her eyes tightly closed.

". . . decapitated during the War. But a great admirer of yours, Katy love, a very great admirer. And a dear friend. Katy, I'd like you to meet my old and excellent ex-commander, Colonel . . . *No, Katy, don't open your eyes!*" Blight whipped out his handkerchief, and took a giant step toward her. With swift and practiced fingers he blindfolded her. She felt his voice whispering warmly in her ear. "The Major carried your photograph into every battle. I hope you understand. One may not refuse a hero . . ."

". . . One may not assume the pathology of another," the physician was saying in a paternal voice, speaking from his responsible position behind his handsome oak and silver-leaf desk. He smiled winsomely, but Blight continued impassive. He offered a cigarette, but Blight preferred snuff. The doctor then tried a firmer tack.

"See here, my dear Blight, one does not make common property of those daydreams, nightmares, those abominable though perfectly normal secrets which ordinary decency demands we deny and keep secret. You are indulging in *folie à deux*, sir. Forgive me for putting it so baldly, but it's the sort of thing that simply isn't done. I must warn you, sir, and God knows, I am no prude." The doctor paused here to accept any challenge, but Blight, bored to tears, blinked twice. The doctor, thus encouraged, continued with his unsolicited professional opinionations.

"Now, I am not setting myself up as a paragon of deadly virtues. Why, I dare say I have the same number of dirty dreams as the next fellow. I am aware that my feces stink no less than yours. I admit to an odd eccentricity or ten. And certainly I must acknowledge my share of illicity in the overall community outrage. But, Blight, my goodness, one must never go so far as to reinforce another's folly. And for one in a position of public trust, there is the added responsibility of correcting and denying these fantasies, these . . ."

"Doctor, I am double-parked." Blight cuts through paper, glass, grease, monotonous voices, gets small talk done with quickly. "Not to be abrupt, Doctor Gnaw, but you understand that I am not treating the public, I am converting my wife. Now, if you don't mind, your signature on that prescription, Doctor, if you please."

> This is the way the truth is told,
> Truth is told, Truth is told.
> This is the way the truth is told,
> A syllable at a time.

It takes great patience to read in Magick, and even greater patience to do it. Scholars and Adepts will comprehend the practical assistance of chemical agents, and will doubtless commiserate in common with Blight, over the necessity of forming unfortunate associations with medicals and other mercenaries. Definitely not the sort of chaps that a gentleman would wish to deal with. Still, certain ingredients are essential in propagating the Mystique. Certain ingredients, difficult to come by . . . the lengths to which one must go in obtaining them. Blight's colleagues will understand.

Chemicals, sleight of hand, misdirection: many devices concurrently employed.

⚔

"Spenser, could I be a man and you the woman, just for one night?"

*

"Darling Spenser, do think of some way we can make ourselves invisible, and then just curl up and watch . . ."

*

"Spenser Angel, what do you suppose there is past passion? I mean, do you think that there is any more, or do you just go back to the end of the line and start all over again?"

*

"Spenser, can't we go a little further? Just a tiny drop further?"

*

"A little further, please . . . ?"

*

"Further . . . ?"

*

And ultimately, that seer question:

"*Spenser, just how far can we go?*" That famous, old, ever magick question. Answer it and die. Or get a girl like Katy to die for you.

But, careful, lest she be all too willing. . . .

Katy insisted that her licentious nature came from a puberty and early adolescence spent in scratchy undergarments. These, her father had firmly believed, were absolutely essential in the training program he had devised for making perfectly devoted little handmaidens out of very young daughters.

Silk the Seducer! The old man had his iron quirks. Neither would he permit her to wear nylon, rayon, or any of the silken substitutes which constituted a serious threat to the modesty that her father had his own peculiar reasons for prizing. Never-you-mind, the old Papa knew exactly what he was about.

Silk was directly responsible for the voluptuous conduct so prevalent among the children of our overly lenient age. Children let to run where they please, undisciplined, unleashed. Children let out-of-doors, to laugh or cry as they choose, with never a thought for their parent's pleasure, with never a moment for their parent's amusement.

Katy's Daddy had rules against the selfishness of children. Most ingenious rules. They could be fastened to metal rings set in the wall, and left chained like that for as many days as it took each time to humble a proud and arrogant child. With special punishment diets of tepid water and stale bread, served in the dog's dish on the cement floor of the Bad Girl Room.

But, despite her father's piety and his precautions, despite his sudden and unannounced Underwear Examinations: the abrupt command to lift her skirts . . . the penalty for disobedience being twice the penalty for wearing unauthorized unmentionables, or sixteen strokes with a willow wand cut while it was green, or a like number from a budding birch rod. Daddy had several ways of counting, and every one of them made her shriek.

But none of them could prevent her from exchanging the coarse gray woolen bloomers that her Papa so favored for the forbidden sleazys that she begged, borrowed, and stole; then wore against her skin till it was time for Dad to catch her and make her lift her skirt.

"*Higher. Show what you are wearing . . . so!*" Then Daddy would call for his whips, for his equipment, his complicated correction paraphernalia . . . with which he developed Katy's silken appetites to such an outstanding and well-publicized degree that we are not surprised that her name has become synonymous with prosperity on half the mulberry farms of the world, and silk merchants keep her picture on the walls of their offices.

And although she lived long enough to be one of the six witnesses to her father's flaming death, and though she had no less than five pounds of lingerie at any given moment of her adult life; though she traveled constantly, leaving complete wardrobes as well as nearly whole people behind, never did she discard that curious article of under-attire; that stiff, ugly, prison-gray garment of her childhood. The bloomers that Daddy used to make her wear. She showed them many times to Spenser, pointing out, with something like pride, the padded crotch laced with horsehair stitching. The old man's doing. Undergarments with a crotch, custom-cut and resewn to insure the maximum irritation to that sensitive area where dwells a maiden's modesty, her imps, her dolls, and all the fortune she can span. . . .

Katy was magnificent. Dressed in a gown of emerald green. Stylishly short, the hem broke three inches above her silken knee. She wore pointy, green shoes, covered with the same material as her gown and set off by silver heels, five and a half inches high. Her midnight hair was swept back from her forehead and kept in place by seven pearl-headed pins. A choker of pearls encircled her neck: pale beads lying against her luminous flesh.

The plunging V, the low-cut bodice, the extremely daring

scoop will always be in racy fashion, if not in the best of taste. Still Katy insisted on fretting. "You're positive that it's not *too* extreme?" she questioned. Blight reassured. And she was easily, though only temporarily mollified.

"Alright darling, if you think so. If you really think so." Her bosom nearly exposed, perfuming the bedroom of their hotel suite with the fragrance of her breasts. She had just washed her long hair; a masseuse had spent the afternoon rubbing her body; her thighs had been powdered, her mind deranged, in preparation for their evening out.

Katy held her arms out stiffly. Without comment, Spenser drew a pair of long kid leather gloves over them. Gloves, leather gloves, stained rouge red, they were ever so tight, and naturally they must fit without a wrinkle.

Tight, tight! Would you believe it, so extraordinarily tight that she must first coat her bare arms with French chalk before Spenser can work them on. Gloves that swallow her arms from lacquered fingertips to her moist, freshly shaved armpits.

No wonder it took Spenser better than half an hour to finish with the tiny, mother-of-pearl buttons; forty-nine of them on each arm. It was the first time that he had used a button-hook. Exquisite instrument.

Then, from a pocket inside his dinner jacket, he produced a *second pair* of gloves, these very different from the first. Jet black and cut from coarse, stiff leather hide, machine-stitched: so ugly. They put one in mind of those false gloves once worn by amputees. Katy tried to wriggle her fingers. A metal snap fastened the gloves at her wrists. She gasped.

"Can you?" Spenser watched her closely. "Can you move your arms?"

She shook her head. "There's no feeling at all." She gave him a fleeting, rueful smile. "They're numb," she admitted. "You were right. My arms are gone." And in their place, two leather appendages, a double pair of gloves, they might have been stuffed with cotton ticking. "Are you really taking me out in public . . . like this?"

"Without the slightest hesitation." He went to the closet. Katy was studying herself in a full-length mirror, turning this way, then that way. Blight returned with their wraps; he draped a fur stole over her shoulders. "Why shouldn't we go anywhere we please? My darling, surely you don't imagine that anyone would be unkind to such a stunning cripple as yourself?"

Blight was quite right. Of course.

They enjoyed a celebrity's stroll cross town. Sidewalk crowds parted as they approached. The people fell back, according Katy the deference and surreptitious curiosity usually reserved for hunchbacked queens, or mutilated heroines, sole survivors of some recent Congo massacre.

Their demeanor was sufficient to fluster a first-class maitre d' into escorting them to a prominent table in an expensive, well-lit, and rather crowded restaurant. There, they ate—a delicious, painstaking performance—a complete dinner, from cocktails to coffee. And not once was their appetite disturbed by the slightest intrusion. Whenever they happened to glance up from their fun, it mildly amused them to note that every eye was looking the other way.

Spenser had pulled his chair next to Katy's, the better to attend to her. That magnificent oddment, Blight's Katy. She sat at her place, stiff, ramrod straight. Her leather-sheathed arms, with their double-dead hands lay on either side of her plate, exactly as Blight had arranged them at the beginning of their meal. She was a young, big-breasted, exceptionally luscious and full-hipped woman, a beauty with two lifeless arms buttoned up tight in long, reddish shrouds, with a shiny black hood snapped snugly around each immobile hand.

"Spenser, I'm so terribly thirsty. Mayn't I have a sip of wine?"

Blight gazed at her fondly. A total dependent. One can appreciate his rapture. It was apparent to the entire restaurant. If not for Spenser, who would have lifted the wineglass to her puckering, tangerine-shaded lips? How should the unfortunate creature have managed had not Spenser cut up her meat, exactly as one does for a very small child? But no child this . . . Katy. She was a lush, fruited-mouth beauty with smoke-grey eyes. A great beauty. But helpless. And she must be fed a forkful at a time.

"Don't dribble," Blight cautioned her.

All around the restaurant, trained nurses, at least one at every table, leaned forward and licked their lips as Blight lifted the wineglass; holding it as one would hold a flower, by its stem, teasing and tickling his nice, ripe cripple.

"Open your mouth, Katy."

She did as he told her to: that was part of the magick part. She opened her mouth and tilted her head, and her eyes begged as he tipped the wineglass higher and higher. Her throat worked convulsively. Blight smiled hugely and Katy's eyes grew wider, more and more frantic. *Please don't!* She gagged, and Spenser, aware that everyone was watching her, watching him, proved himself more than equal to the occasion. He took the honors by a sly and successful threat, a most innocuous intimidation, done right in front of a restaurant full of big eyes. It was precious.

He merely put down the wineglass and lifted her napkin from her lap to her lips, and held it there, making his intention perfectly clear. *Swallow it. Don't dare lose a drop . . . or would you rather your lipstick were smeared most dreadfully? And that is just what will happen if you drool. I will use this napkin to wipe your lipstick all over your face* said his eyes.

The wine went down in one great gulp. Her mouth

twisted, but she kept it down. And heard everyone whisper, *Poor girl.* Or was that just egomania and high blood pressure? The napkin had rather unsettled her. She had some idea of the things that Spenser could do with a napkin. She had played one or two of those things before . . . had him wipe her lipstick across her face, and then insist upon repairing the damage. Right then and there. And she would have had to let him. When else but right then, and where else but right there? What else could he have done, had he chosen (as he very nearly had!) to repaint her mouth, while a restaurant, packed with slimy tongues and sneak-thief eyes, slavered and popped? The thought of it was more than enough to make her bare shoulders prickle. And it had very nearly happened to her. That was the best part. Katy shivered. She had only *just* managed to down the wine. She had just barely escaped some awful and humiliating moments, she didn't doubt it. Moments long, while she must sit still as a dummy; grimacing, puckering, preening at his command, while he fussed and teased with her makeup. O and never would he permit her a mirror; she knew that he wouldn't. He would force her to sit there, till he was done, till he'd had his pleasure; till the end, she would remain a cripple of his, on display.

And all the while, she, poor girl, would not even be allowed to know what her own face looked like.

Her left arm twitched slightly in an indiscreet gesture that aborted under Blight's alert forefinger. He pressed the metal snap at her wrist, and her arm withered and fell off again.

"I was thinking about that time on the train from Philadelphia, when you kept changing my makeup from one clown face to another." Katy's eyes were glassy. "I still get scared when I remember . . . Oh, those terrible, big red lips that you kept drawing on me. And that word you wrote on my forehead. Can you imagine . . . if someone had seen us!"

"You would have loved it . . . you extravagant exhibitionist!"

". . . am not! It was you!" was all she could blurt out before he had stuffed a heaping forkful of mashed potatoes into her mouth. And their playful dinner continued.

Can you name the game? More important, do you play . . . ?

Would you? That is, could you, if you so desired?

Are you satisfied that you feel enough, or is there any sort of chance that you might just possibly be interested in feeling something more?

Was there reason to believe that Blight and Katy, under the guise of eating out, were, in actuality, dining in; nourishing themselves on secret tidbits, developing all sorts of interior powers, eating all sorts of mysteries, and feeling more than most people? Going further, feeling forces, perceiving influences that didn't exist.

Love is an example. Where is it? Find it? Feel it?

What do you suppose it is like . . . seated beside your beloved, you reach out, *and discover that you have no arms.* . . .

. . . a ripple of pure pleasure was the phrase used by Katy in her journal to describe *the sensation of total restraint,* as she remarks it elsewhere in those curious diaries. *The tingle that comes only when securely tied. That, and the other things too.* . . . At times, Katy comes very close to giving away the trade secrets. Still, it's thanks owed to Katy for her pioneering experiments which have so materially contributed to the shedding of light upon the role played by mortification, its utilization and possible contraindications, in the science of psychic phenomena.

The motivations for her investigations may be examined elsewhere. The results are given here.

Or would you have it that Katy was a victim? Is anything quite *that* simple?

What, do you suppose, you would have to give to tempt a beautiful, young, just-married heiress to throw away her arms? Obviously, one must offer something better than arms. Think on it, but be warned, it's a puzzle that poisons.

Be quick. Be Blight and outmaneuver Katy. Or be Katy, and enjoy the benefits of being outmaneuvered. See it or be it, that's up to you. Attendance at Blight's demonstrations is not compulsory.

But just in case somebody should be watching. . . .

Blight lights two cigarettes. He hooks the waiter with his eye, and as the man hurries over, Blight puts one of the cigarettes in his own mouth; the other one he puts between Katy's lips. And he gets her again.

Katy doesn't smoke.

And now comes the best part of their act: the sort of thing that one could see all day long, and all night too, but because of magick, does not see it at all. Or only very rarely.

Look here . . . Katy is coughing violently. The cigarette falls into her lap, and her right breast pops out of its low-slung bra cup. Just as the waiter arrives with the check.

What to do? Quick the trick, or else the waiter will gasp and blow the whistle to let the entire restaurant know for a fact that Katy's teat is hanging out, and that her lap is really burning. That's enough for a riot. More than enough to provoke an altercation with anyone of the many, many envious Magis present. At the very least, could Blight hope to escape with less than a Freqk-Snatcher's unwelcome intrusion? Some dog would be sure to bark, FIRE! and hurry over with a pitcher of ice water.

But Blight's there first.

His expression is impeccable, impenetrable: he uses it to screen his incredibility. With his left hand he pushes Katy's right breast back into its emerald bodice, and with his right hand he pinches out the little spurt of flame in her lap. Quick as that. Kitchee-Koo.

And he's back in time to lift the check from the silver tray. His eye runs down the column of figures, his cigarette still dangling from the side of his mouth. Blight glances up. Blows a thin stream of smoke past the waiter's blank face. He'd seen nothing. He didn't dare see anything. . . .

"Change for a fifty," Blight said, and it was over. Opera lovers all over the restaurant applauded, swooned, threw secret bouquets as Blight received his change, rose to his full height. He snapped his fingers and Katy reacted immediately. She got to her feet with an acrobat's grace: this snake-hipped woman, all in green satin and two shades of leather. This tall, young, volatile woman, with her rare, inviting expression, and her magnetic body. Everyone stared. Everyone held their breath as she followed him: Blight and Katy, threading their way in and out of the maze of tables, across the floor to the cloakroom, where she waited, patient as the Sphinx, while a curly-headed blond attendant searched for their wraps.

'Twas lookity-look, and O look at that! Dinners got cold and wine turned to vinegar while the diners, the waiters, the busboys, and cigarette girls, everyone in the restaurant, all stared in the other direction . . . all peeked around the corner of their eyes, to see the last of Katy and her dreadful arms, dead in their leather casings, hanging at her sides like leaden weights.

Now Blight covered his wife's bare blushing shoulders with her fur. A seven-foot doorman, dressed like a Cossack, leapt out of nowhere and flung the street door open with a royal flourish.

"Yes sir! Taxi for you and the lady, sir?"

"Not this evening, thank you," said Blight, and taking one of Katy's dead arms, he escorted her through the open door; tipping the enthusiastic Cossack a wiggle and a wave from Katy's bright green backside, they made their quaint way up the street and into the night.

IV

Bloated old Blight, he eats next to nothing, yet each time he weighs himself he's grown a gross pound or two grosser.

The impressive dome, lowered; the desklight breaking on the bald skull, shedding light on the long and curious scar, dead white, it burns from the slight depression of the crown to the base of the external occipital protuberance, less than an inch above his soiled collar. Within that excessively convoluted cranium, a rare incubelum bubbles: a brain mash of memories and myths and bits of Blightclerk lore, wherein the truth is indistinguishable from desire. And desire is drawn from the loose ends of dreams, there for the taking, untagged and un-regarded, waiting for anyone in the public domain. And Blight wanders through, picking and choosing the parts he likes best.

Take from this one a pound, add two pinches of this, a dram of that. Here take this arm, and those eyebrows. Tear only a few fingers off from that, and the foot . . . Blight's no packrat. He's no fat greedy. He salvages only the parts that fit

His Master-Plan

assembled from other plans. Whole paragraphs that suit his motif are lifted from their surrounding wordage, intact, and ingested into Blight. His stomach juices burn out the memories of origins, and all his words swear allegiance to James Spenser Blight. And those who don't believe it are invited to watch how a Specialist makes himself up. Watch the Nightclerk string all his beads on a single, obsessive thread.

"Oh Jim, it certainly was thrilling!" cried Jill, kissing him. Then she called Gwendoline, la petite upstairs maid. "Oh Gwen, now it is your turn!" she cried, brushing some crumbs off the other girl's starched bosom. "Now you can have some fun with the Baroness Von Kai!" cried Jill, and she handed Gwendoline the feather . . .

. . . A voice, not Spenser's, read aloud from the book of dirty thumbprints: a paperbound novel which lay on the desk, covers spread and the pages exposed to shameless, vagrant breezes loitering in the pre-dawn lobby.

A GIRL'S STRANGE STORY

An obscene classic. A classic obscenity. The wind snickers and turns the pages, two at a time.

> after this experiment. Now the Baroness lay still, completely under the influence of the Herr Doktor's mysterious, colorless, odorless, tasteless drug. Her matchless Prussian bosom rose and fell with a regular, measured, and subtly hypnotic rhythm.
>
> "Now?" panted the gorgeous Georgina. "Now please O please may I throw the switch?"
>
> The Herr Docktor ran the stump of his index finger thoughtfully along the old dueling scar. He feasted on the prone body of the Baroness, strapped to his operating table. Then his eyes, big icy disks behind his thick, rimless glasses, slid coldly across the laboratory to where the patient but beautiful Georgina, her hand trembling on the Master Switch-Control, waited for his permission.
>
> "Ja!" he gave it with a sneer and the depraved Georgina squeaked ecstatically as she jerked the

Nightclerk mumbled in his sleep, and the voice broke off abruptly, as a wind of warning whispered, *Shhhhh.* But too late.

Blight moved from dreams to wakefulness with practiced agility. He had heard the voice and he had recognized the text. The blimp dome lifted, and the Nightclerk's amber eyes slid coolly from the dream on his lap to the novel lying open on the desk. The breezes hastened to cover their indiscretion; airy fingers ruffled the pages, but Blight only sneered. As if one had simply to lose the place, confuse the issue, only turn the page to escape.

In a voice curdled with contempt, almond bitter, and loud enough to make the cobwebs flutter, the Nightclerk mocked from memory:

> ecstasy as she jerked the lever that turned the contact key that sent the triple XXX power coursing joyously into the parallel conductors that supplied the force to activate the magnetic hands built by the brilliant but beautiful Herr Doktor to get his revenge.

The lobby glared furiously, but kept a guilty silence. The Nightclerk glared back. He cleared his throat with a harsh, wet growl and spat accurately into the trashbasket beside the desk. Two fat fingers searched his vest pockets for the snuff box. The phantoms remained at bay, their tails between their legs. (Later, they would creep up and lick the few grains of snuff that might have spilled around the custom-built, well-padded swivel chair. But now, with the Nightclerk watching them, they kept just out of sight.) For his part, Blight would not dignify them by further notice. It was unseemly for Blight . . . James Spenser Blight, who, after all, was a man who in the course of a single afternoon, had gained four hundred and forty-nine pounds, and lost every single hair on his blessed head. Is it likely that such a man would be much troubled by lobby ghosts, by dusty shadows creeping around the decrepit furniture? And though he sits as long as the best of them, does anyone see any dust on Blight?

There's swaybacked couches and spavined divans, there's ottomans and settees, whole suites of whorehouse furnishings, many, many brothel parlors piled into one cavern, which is under the authority of one Nightclerk. A single, indivisible Nightclerk. And his name, for the time being, is James Spenser Blight. And he is in charge of this great, sagging, amortorium.

Now he laces his hands across the celebrated expanse, the

Blightian belly. Now the naked dome, the great bald shield, is lowered again, and the yellow eyes turn inward, once more.

The Nightclerk may his hotel rule, but who has power over the hotel's shadows? Who can stay them from their unfriendly business, their tricks, and their appointed wicked deeds? Who can guess what they are up to, the instant one lowers his head or closes his eyes? And just how far will they be allowed to go before a stop is put to their vexations?

A Nightclerk's functions include directing each guest to his box; making certain that the maids have changed the sand, washed the bedsprings, wiped off the fingerprints. That sort of thing. He is expected to protect Smith from Jones, the fourth floor from the fifth, the anonymity of those falsely registered, as well as the *de facto* autonomy of their enemies, bad dreams, the social diseases, and beggars from the Bi-Sex Squad. Of course, a Nightclerk can only do his best, and no one should be very surprised if he loses a few guests per shift.

And here it is altogether appropriate to note, without any desire to blow Blight's golden horn, but purely in the service of our Lady Truth, Blight's safety score is third from highest. A fair measure of the degree of excellence with which he discharged his duties, and the competence with which he executed his responsibilities.

So how was it possible to blame him for the vaguely threatening figures, the faintly familiar shapes flickering just off-frame? Can there really be doctors who believe that Blight is the *fons et origo* of these phantasticals? Or are we witnessing another Inquisition, a repetition of the Witch and Wizard Burnings of Lidice, Salem, and Warsaw? Is one not put in mind of the Nuremberg Trials, the rabid mouthings of John of Weirus, de Lorenzo, Mather . . . the whole disreputable rabble of Foul Liars, Charlatans, and Anti-Semites?

Yes, we have heard from these False Prophets before. Now we hear them again, hear them curse Blight and deny their own existence in the very same sentence. See you their double game?

Otherwise intelligent men are beguiled into error and give the world away because the ghosts have persuaded them there is no such thing. There is only a Nightclerk, so say these ghosts. The only mystery is why a fat, disgusting, bald, and probably dangerous old man is left in charge, all night long. . . .

Don't listen!

Intelligent men . . . why do you withhold your support from Nightclerks who are trained to watch over you? Why do you go instead, with your life in your hands, to the alleys and grub-end streets where black cats wait to get your tongue?

Use that tongue to save yourself. And start by saving your Nightclerk. For if he goes, where shall you find a bed at night? And what would please the ghosts more . . . than a city full of wakeful people?

Will this happen to *your* city?

Don't ask Blight. He's no comfort to anyone. He has already gone so far as to give his opinion that there are ghosts, and that there are no ghosts. For the benefit of those who need every question answered twice, he will repeat that the Dead, although they may very well be buried, still they may rise and walk the streets at night.

He will not enlarge upon this statement. He will discuss it no further. And as for the voices, this he *absolutely refuses* to comment on. . . .

. . . Although he will say this much:

While it is true there are no ghosts, there are, however, voices which have routed more than one solitary from his innocent and much needed sleep. Voices, which have made him to open his eyes in 3 A.M. lobbies, in the close air of rented rooms, in lonely beds, and in darkened buses speeding through the anxious night.

And there the matter stands. Carve it any way you will. There are no ghosts, but there are voices which constantly disturb the peace. Voices whispering just outside the window, or just on the other side of the wall.

Answer your own question . . . or did you never wake at an apprehensive hour, in a narrow, desperate bed, and hear the conspiratorial tones of a voice that you can almost remember. A voice telling your name and where you buried the body. And to whose hands the blood doth cling.

No great wonder that men prefer to deny the whole thing, and huddle with the bedclothes up around their ears. Who wouldn't rather swear that he hears nothing . . . ? Nothing at all.

And still the voices go on whispering.

Who exposed himself in the park, and who was it molested the deaf and dumb child, foolishly left to play by herself, in a desolate thicket outside the playground?

Who asks these questions. . . ? And who answers them in that dreadful, sibilant, that soft and O so guilty whisper that can be heard around the world, destroying the sleep of intelligent men everywhere?

Why should this be permitted? Why should a man be awakened at 3 A.M. by ghosts or gas or neighbors quarreling across the airshaft? Whether it be imagination, indigestion, or wicked spirits . . . who wants to wake up and hear voices telling all the secrets, financial, social, marital, medical, even criminal secrets, to the thousands and thousands of other men, all strangers and potential rivals, lying around in their bad beds, locked in their lonesome boxes, and scattered throughout the major cities? It is not pleasant to consider that one's most intimate secrets are nightly rehearsed in such remote places as Kiev, in a suburb of Nice, in the center of St. Louis de Ville, in a Melbourne rooming house.

How is it that one always seems to be meeting persons who apparently know more about one than they possibly could? And if not ghosts, then well and good, but may we wonder what little birdie has been telling tales? Who is to blame for ruining your sleep and mine with gratuitous information that either exposes us, or renders us accessories to abominations that we never had any intention of committing?

If not ghosts, then who do you imagine it is that gloats, that chortles, that describes our most embarrassing moments, our most repugnant activities in such vivid, disgusting, and extended detail? Who prattles? Who tattles? Who digs up things that were buried for a reason?

Who fills the dawn with fog and dread?

To the point: there are no ghosts, but no man's life is safe from voices. While he sleeps they tell his everything. And he wakes a bankrupt, ruined, disgraced. . . .

. . . So, while all are agreed that there are no ghosts, there remains a wide division of opinion regarding the great demand for competent magickians, and the huge market for enchantments to keep the secrets safe, the voices silent. And to this end, whole fields are given up to growing poppies. And in this cause, mountebanks, diverting clowns, court fools, and their like, are raised to positions high in the sky, are laved with love, and get adored for their skill and ability to make our life with ghosts at least possible.

Blight, you may be quite sure, concurs with the Experts. There are no ghosts. There are only millions of people going to the movies, taking barbiturates, magnetic baths, other nickle & dime pleasures to bring temporary relief.

And when the ghosts persist, as they always do, there's millions of people going to see their doctors, complaining of backaches and asking for something stronger.

At 3:33 in the morning, there's only people lying wide-eyed in bed, wrongdoers creeping close to the walls, and Nightclerks sitting in haunted lobbies. Why devise elaborate narrations?

Why tell everything but the truth?

Downtown, in the lobby of the Travelers Hotel, there is a Nightclerk, a victim of a glandular disorder; a man who is soiled inside and out, and who, at this moment, is settled comfortably in his oversized swivel chair, dozing on his dais, while voices grow more brazen every moment. They discuss his past, pretend to be greatly shocked, threaten to report him, and invariably ask for more details.

They don't fool Blight, neither do they frighten him. In fact, he's grown rather fond of them. In fact, he wouldn't dream of making them hush. See . . . he licks his chops. They must be telling a good part now.

Who would have guessed that Blight was so devoted to his voices? Not that there's any shame in that, as any man who ever worked the nightshift will testify. The memory goes—why shouldn't it? And one begins to confuse a long-ago conversation with a long-ago deed that never was done, only discussed. But it's hard to be sure. And the keepsakes have been misplaced, old letters are lost, old friends are gone, and new acquaintances are no use at all. Then where should a Nightclerk get his past if not from the phantoms whose delight it has always been to spy upon him, to follow him everywhere, to peek over his shoulder, to witness his adventures, to review his lurid case? Without voices, where should a Nightclerk find words to fill in the blanks between the few odd bones of memories? A pigtail wrapped in yellow silk, a pair of false eyelashes. Such distantly related bits as one manages to snatch from the fires, to salvage from the tribute-hungry years. Without his voices, what should he make of this note, this message, carried like a talisman in his wallet . . . this wallet found on the chancy side-walk, eleven or nine years ago. Was this message, writ in tangerine-shaded lipstick, on the paper napkin from some restaurant called

Mama Lion's

Cocktails & Fine Food

Closed Mondays

part of the wallet that Blight had picked off the street, or was it part of his personal collection . . . most of which has since been scattered. Gainsaying the note which he's saved in his wallet. Or which he found there.

Blight doesn't worry. Let the voices decide on a truth. Let them give their interpretation of this unsolicited communication. Obviously written by a woman, left handed, and in a hurry. More than that was the sheerest sort of conjecture. Just wishful thinking.

One might as well seek meaning in mice droppings as to attempt a recollection, a reconstruction, a satisfactory explanation of messages writ with *any* color lipstick, with an eyebrow pencil, a match stick dipped in mascara. Always doubt documents done in cosmetics.

It takes a ghost to really remember. . . .

It worked. Have gone with him. Fascin'ting develops. Xpect my call, midnite @ our hotel. If I can. Love + Kisses

Let the voices gather around the roomdesk, and let them tell Blight all his favorite stories while the lobby draws closer and the night ticks away. A reputable Nightclerk has every right to his voices. He cannot be expected to cut magazines and read dreadful novels all night long. It is intolerable to imagine that a Nightclerk must do *all* the dreaming that needs to be done in a six-story hotel.

And no further apologies need be made for Blight's addiction to phantasmata. And further questions will not be answered. Not by Blight. Henceforth, he is willing to let his voices speak for him.

Are you willing to listen?

Blight is elsewhere. Occupied with other matters. He's off tasting the dainties that he put aside hundreds of years ago, against these nights of his fat and hateful old age.

Save your pity. Other Diabolicals, past their prime, flat-footed and unlovely: they've lost their teeth, and they get no dessert because they subsist on Charity, the quality of which is definitely strained, and in any case, will not pay for custard pudding and chocolate cupcakes.

Blight is better off than they. In the time of his magick he had the good sense to save a few apples, to keep them vacuum-packed and cellophane-wrapped in brown aspho leaves. Blight doesn't worry. He can retire to Florida anytime he wants to.

Yes. There is such a thing as eating your past and having it too! It's one of those secrets that money can't buy, that no skill can win, that your most adept alchemist may not counterfeit. It is one of those Mysteries which all men covet, but which only a true Blight would take in his mouth.

And there is no other way to do this trick. Swallow it or lose it. Nightclerks must follow some of the same rules as everyone else.

Two big fingers, thumb and index, creep out of Blight's sleep and tug at his collar. His neck itches and his dreams are strangling him. Again.

What nonsense. There are no dreams, nor are there any rules. There is only an old Blight, told and retold, lashed to his swivel chair; a gallant and doomed Nightclerk, prepared to go down with his night. Or would you see him as an exceedingly fat man napping, secure in his chins and confident that eventually this train too will leave? And that his ticket is tucked into his vest pocket. Anytime they want it, they can have it.

Hazards of the profession. Stigmata and other medals, and mentions honorable, ribbons awarded for clerical duties above and beyond the Protective Circle. Professional tributes paid to a man who night, after night, exposed himself

to danger.

Not only is it dangerous, it is also disgusting for men to live alone. They dissolve into such piggish habits. Their closets fill up with their soiled underwear and their dirty socks. They leave puddles in the bathroom: their old gray truss hangs from the convenient doorknob. They seem not to notice: apparently they don't mind . . . that the world is peeling off in strips. The fabric tears even as the hand is reaching for it. Old men living old lives alone; they go their sad way, and after the buttons have all fallen off, they fasten their shirts with safetypins, with string, with whatever is handy. Gristle from their gray beards sticks to the shaving soap; and though their heads be as bald as their palms, still, long dark hairs appear regularly, pasted around the sides of the sink . . . combed out, over some other sink in some other long-ago bathroom. These long and magickal hairs that have crawled like fairy eels, crawled through a million sewer systems, crawled through time to rendezvous here in the old man's sink; here at the end of the long, long pipe, the hairs slither forth to trouble and mystify absent-minded old duffers, who stand in front of their basins. Often with a razor in their hand. Rarely with any good reason why not.

And on top of the medicine cabinet, there're more razor blades, rusting out of sight. These are sometimes called *invisible presentiments,* or *unseen apprehensions.* Only a very few old men have any idea of what is troubling them.

They keep their cells in monstrous disorder, all the while maintaining the most elaborate rituals, which never seem to be elaborate enough to calm the old men, to clean their stalls, to send the hairs back to where they came from. Despite the rituals, or because of them, the chaos continues; things get worse and worse, despite and/or because of all sorts of abnormal behavior and regular magick done by solitary old men in the desperate hope of bringing some semblance of regularity into their crazy, intemperate lives.

Old men, they do magick for nothing more than a good night's sleep.

Who cares why old men do what they have to? Who cares that some must go without food in order to buy the magick, without which they would surely die of disappointment, neglect, gout, disengagement. Without magick how should they survive even the ordinary abrasions that one sustains in the normal hit and run of everyday on earth?

As a gentleman grows older, his bruises no longer heal as quickly or as completely as once upon a time they did. A gentleman, if he lives long enough, might conceivably find himself in considerable pain. Some old gentlemen have found it necessary to double their magick, and so attempt to treat themselves with massive overdoses. Others simply can't afford to use so much.

In any event, we all grow older, sooner or later. Older, fatter, balder. A gentleman may very well reach the point where he goes out less and less, and is most comfortable only in his own company. There is suddenly so much to occupy him: he's kept so busy digging arrowheads and other indian relics out of the soft clay of his past. Finding all sorts of things he can't remember having buried in the fertile fields around the thalamus. He finds pottery, household articles, part of a plow, a section of a sword. Each day brings new artifacts to the surface, uncovers new evidence. Each day's digging offers a chance to reshape his history, revise old and less than satisfactory recollections. Meanwhile he grows fatter, paler, more preoccupied. The long hairs continue to clog his basin. He finds recourse in detestable intercourse, and he has more and more to do with succubi and web-footed women: females of no certain species. He buys his magick at Thrift Shops and Secondhand Stores. Sometimes it works, more often it doesn't. More often the old man is left to his own devices, his own delusions, his faulty perceptions which tempt him to wander further back into his skull. Eventually to disappear entirely. To be posted on the Forever Missing List. His property seized, and his rooms re-rented. His corpse hacked up by freshmen surgeons learning at their slabs, one-two-three-four-five all in a row.

Foxy Grandpaws, and sour Recluses, middle-aged Fops, Hermits, Paupers, Solitaries of every affection, and just plain Dirty Old Men . . . they drop like flies on every side. Dead in the wind, dead in the tall grass, dead before the trees turn brown.

Nightclerks vanish like everyone else. They are entitled to privileged treatment only so long as they remember their names, their numbers, their enchantments, and how they came into their Nightclerkmanships. So long as they can recall themselves, are positive of the important dates and places; so long as they remain intact they cannot be harmed, or disappeared by evil spirits. BUT, should they forget, should they begin to slip . . . a Nightclerk, no less than any man, will bleed when cut. His bones are breakable. If skinned alive, or boiled in oil, he'll scream, he'll plead: he'll not be so high and mighty then.

It's all well and good for Spenser to go around and around in his bald head, giving in to this and that, containing himself within the inner night. When it suits him, in his great good time, he permits himself to be seduced by men wearing women's faces. He operates the switchboard, he threatens the guests; he struggles with his terrible temper, and curbs his desire to punish. And contents himself with deciding who shall sleep this night, and who shall not.

A most moderate Nightclerk in every respect. He is above reproach . . . but not out of danger. Any man of single passion, any one basket containing all the eggs, any double-or-nothing player is a perpetual calamity getting ready to happen.

Any lover like Blight, who finds his greatest delight in hybrid couplings and unusual courtships; any Nightclerk who spends half his off-duty hours going around to the rooms rented to the hot-pillow trade—unoccupied in the bright, daylight hours—and turning on the bureau mirrors so that he may watch reruns of last night's fun: the troopers astride their winded whores, the Boys galloping their noble doxies. . . .

How long had Blight been at it? How many years had he served? How many days had he turned into night? How many women had he made into men, and how many men had he unmanned?

Blight had no desire to count the number of razor blades on top of *his* medicine cabinet. He had done that yesterday. Only yesterday, but today he couldn't recall how many.

Alright. There it is. The Truth, out in the open at long

last. Here's the rotten apple in the big barrel; the soft spot where most Nightclerks slip. Blight weighed six hundred and fourteen pounds, and here the ice was very thin.

Very thin indeed, for overweight Nightclerks who couldn't remember, who couldn't recall. . . .

. . . whether it had been Katy or himself who had first thought of taking the child into the shower with them.

"O wouldn't that be a funny thing to do! What a grand time we will have!" He still could hear either his voice or Katy's, promising the little girl. "O just imagine, taking a real shower with all your clothes on!"

"Mommy wouldn't let me." The child was so demure.

"We won't tell Mommy," Spenser swore and placed his hand on the child's golden head. "Your Mommy won't be back until Wednesday, and nobody has to know . . ."

"Cross my heart and hope to die," Katy added her blessings. "We can dry your clothes on the stove, and I'll iron your dress. Mommy won't ever know."

("Oh Li'l White Blossom!" the Chinese nurse, Meh Nug, had kissed her fingers a few hours previous, when she'd delivered her charge to Blight. "Li'l White Blossom . . . Li'l Lucy. An' only twelve years old! Only twelve. . . !")

"Drink your champagne, dear, and then we'll all get into the shower together. Just like they do at movie star parties . . ."

"Do I have to finish all my champagne? It makes me kind of sleepy." More than anything in the whole, wide, wondering world, little Lucy wanted to be in the movies. And if a famous Film Producer like Mr. Spenser wanted to take a shower with her and Miss Katy, his famous Talent Scoutress, even though it sounded awful strange . . . "Is it alright if I take my shoes off?"

"Of course, dear." Spenser went on stroking her head.

Miss Katy offered her arm to lean on, while Lucy took off first one shoe and then the other.

(Meh Nug had obviously taken pains to dress the child for the occasion. Lucy wore a short white frock with seven fussy petticoats under the immaculate skirt. She wore navy-blue knee socks and white dancing-school shoes that buckled on the side. Her honey-blond hair had been pulled back into a choirgirl's bun.)

"There! Thank you very much, Miss Katy." Little Lucy had the best manners of any girl in her class. She was in the eighth grade. She was also very neat. She put both her sweet white shoes, the dear dancing pumps with their modest inch-and-a-quarter heel, one shoe right next to the other, under the table that held their wineglasses.

The mosaic might be missing a tile or three, but Spenser was not likely to mislay that moment, *the look on Katy's face as Little Lucy bent over.* . . .

Insight is almost always the result of watching the face rather than the backside.

There. That's one detail, precise, sharp, in perfect focus. But as for the twenty-five thousand and ten other details, unhappily, most of them are lost or mutilated past recognition. Here and there a short, blurred scene. The Expert Eye can identify certain persons moving in the fog. . . .

Blight. Without question, that person is Blight.

And it isn't fog, it's steam. Now the other figures fade into focus, and it's Miss Katy, little Lucy, and James Spenser Blight, packed together in a shower stall, hugging each other under a steamy cascade. Katy's *Vermuhjön lichts* frock soaked to her skin. Spenser sopping in his purple pajamas, and the little girl all in white and navy-blue knee socks: as recalled through clouds of steam. Three people playing the always popular

☆☆☆LITTLE LUCY IN THE SHOWER☆☆☆

Playing it
so often that they've worn it out. And now the film is yellow
and cracked and it's hard to see what the people are doing.
It's hard to tell one little Lucy story from another, especially if,
like Spenser, you have seen them all. It's hard to remember
one child star from another. Years and years of double features
dull the faculties, jelly the mind, destroy the only existing
memories of moments that can hardly happen again. If indeed
they ever happened.

With so much activity taking place on the fictive level;
with all the crowds of afterimages coming around years later
and asking for old friends; with cartoons of dreams, and all
those Midnite Shows; all those twelve-year-olds with their big,
startled, innocent, awestruck, childblue eyes . . . .
. . . . **FLASHING ON & OFF & ON & OFF & ON**
the screen, who dares trust Memory? That liar bends both
ways.

And certainly no one in his right mind would expect a
Nightclerk to keep a diary . . . one of those little black books
that make so much trouble for everyone whose name is in it.
If Blight should ever be questioned or searched. . . .

And it could happen. If the Wednesday Outrages continued, anything could and probably would happen. Even
though Blight, all six hundred and twenty-one pounds of
Blight, is firmly committed to the proposition that he will never
stand trial for some crimewave that the ghosts made him to
dream about, and then sent his name to the Police, just to see
what they would do to Blight. Even though he didn't do it, it
didn't matter. Any more than it mattered whether he had his
eyes open or closed when these atrocities, these atrocious at-
tacks and inexplicable homicides took place. . . .

. . . took place

while Blight was asleep and under the influence of somebody else's dreams.

An interesting theory, perhaps, but it doesn't answer the question as to where Blight was and who saw him there on Wednesday morning last, about 6:00 A.M.

Well, Blight's not such a fool as to answer academic questions. Once such a question is asked, it is checkmated in four moves; and everything that Blight says will be used against him. The only problem, after such a question is asked, is how to die gracefully.

Blight is never without his snuffbox or his poison dart, artfully concealed in a fountain pen. It was ever ready to answer the penultimate question in actions louder than words. If it ever came to that. And any minute it might. . . .

But why should it? Why in this wide and wonderful world would a brutal, 6:00 A.M. rape of a nun sleeping peacefully in her plain cotton shift, at the Convent of Perpetual Passion on Dolorous Street, prompt a policeman to ask harmless old man Blight . . . "Where? How? Why?"

Whoever thinks that Blight carried his poison pen clipped over his heart because he was afraid, is wrong. Blight carried his death because he was in the habit of doing so: this habit honorably acquired years before, when Spenser had trained as a spy. And there certainly was no good reason for him to expect a Police interrogation. So long as a man pays his parking tickets, returns his library books, doesn't walk on the grass, or forget to kiss the Detective-on-Duty, he has no cause to assume that the Police will get funny ideas and come around asking funny questions about starry-eyed young nuns of Wednesday morning last,

when an intruder, apparently entering through a side door, using a wax impression to unlock the door, proceeded to

the Penitence Cells, some distance from the main part of the
Convent. There he found a contrite young nun

> who told police that she woke
> about 6:00 A.M. and found a
> man dressed in a nun's habit
> standing beside her bed. He
> was holding what the Sister
> thought was an eleven-and-a-
> half inch hunting knife. She
> said that he was an extremely
> stout man, but could add little
> more to her description, as
> she had seen him for a second
> or two at most, before she'd
> thrown her arm across her
> face to protect herself from
> the long, slender, gleaming

And then she must have fainted. When she regained consciousness, her head was in a bag. She couldn't see, she couldn't
scream. The man was kneeling on her breasts, crushing the
breath out of her. And the tip of the knife blade pricked her
soft throat.

> "I remember thinking at the
> time, he must be a pious man
> gone wrong," the hospitalized
> nun told interested Detectives.
> "He was mumbling something,
> and while I can't be absolutely
> sure of the words, I did catch
> the rhythm, and I had the dis-
> tinct impression that he was
> saying his prayers. Yes, I
> know that sounds crazy, but it
> was me that he was kneeling
> on. And all the time he was
> kneeling on me, he kept
> mumbling."

Under further questioning, the attractive and still penitent young victim admitted that nothing like this had ever happened to her before, and that it was more than likely that she was mistaken.

In a signed statement, the Sister said in part: "I am sorry but I cannot say for sure how it felt. I was so scared. But I think it felt like a fat man on top of me, praying. And then I fainted again."

Police also took a statement from Eugene White, a fourteen - year - old altarboy, who was sleeping in a room next to the cell where the attack took place.

"I didn't hear or see anything. I am a very, very heavy sleeper," the boy admitted.

Blight, on the other hand, admitted nothing. All he knew was what he read in the newspapers. And it seems—according to the newspapers—that on Blight's night off, some stout man, using Blight's *modus operandi,* unlocked a convent door and violated a nun.

The anticlerical sentiments of Blight are too well documented to require more than a mention here. Further than this, however, we may not presume. Neither is it proper to speculate on the cost of an altarboy's cooperation.

How should Blight know? Is he a man to make a nun into a prayer mat? He categorically denies this and all the crimes committed on his night off. And he will not answer any questions that no one has asked him.

And it isn't likely that anyone will ask. They're far too clever to make the mistake of asking direct questions. They have no intention of allowing any man the opportunity to explain. Why should they encourage alibis, and let any man from off the hook? They much prefer to continue the Innocent and the Guilty, all together, under the same dark cloud. And never are they so pleased as when a Pillar of Society is made to crumble right in front of everybody. They are not so concerned with catching a criminal as they are with inspiring some hapless wretch to empty an ashtray on his own head and run out into the streets screaming his own shame, his secrets, his wife's secrets, any secrets that he can pronounce, so craven do men become when kept too long under the strain of mornings, afternoons, and evenings when there is nothing to do but wait for the Postman to deliver the Accusation, so that the Denial may be filed, and Due Process instigated, and a Final Judgment handed down so that one may once and for all know, past any shadow of a doubt, whether or not he did it.

And there the matter hangs: the sword above the head. The naked sword, the unprotected pate. And it's no great surprise that eventually everyone loses his patience and runs out into the street without his shoes, weeping, wailing, proclaiming his guilt. Waving *Mea Culpa* flags, and chanting: *Guilty, Guilty-O,* in accents lugubrious.

All this guilt, but nobody to tell anybody what they're guilty of. Naturally the Courts are packed with Defendants demanding their right to defend, to go to trial and get cross-examined, and be made to swear, and so forth. Small wonder that half the population is so willing to confess to crimes committed by the other half.

While Blight goes free.

"We'll get him," Lieut. Dearie of the Downtown Detail said in answer to newsmen's questions about the Wednesday Morning Monster. "It's only a matter of time till he gets sick of eating in restaurants," Dearie added confidently. "He'll arrest himself. They always do."

And meanwhile, once a week, in the early hours of every Wednesday morning, a phantom-fiend struck. A woman screamed. But no one ever heard her in time. And there were never any witnesses.

Neither was there any apparent reason to suspect a certain inscrutable Nightclerk. It's all there in Public Record, the newspapers.

Pick a Wednesday, any Wednesday. And what have we here. . . ? Read all about Mrs. Nelly R., 59 years of age, a widow, struck down in Short Lusk Alley, between the hours of 4:45 and 5:15 A.M., on a chilly Wednesday exactly five weeks prior to the Dolorous Street rape.

Is it worth mentioning that the alley, a deserted stretch of cement and broken wine bottles, was a scant two block stroll from the very same hotel where Blight lived and nightclerked? Every A.M. but Wednesday A.M.

Let Nelly explain what she was seeking in an alley at such a forsaken hour. . . . Blight might very well wish for further information, for truth to tell, he really couldn't recall where he'd been when Mrs. Nelly R. got her reward, right in Blight's own neighborhood. The whole truth—and all its attendant treachery—is that Blight drew a blank each and every Wednesday morning. He had to read the newspaper for suggestions of his previous evening's revel. And every Wednesday, there it was. Something new and savage, with no satisfactory explanation. Nobody really seemed to know.

Mrs. Maureen Miller didn't know. Who did it to her. At approximately 5:00 A.M., one week to a Wednesday after Nelly left. Mrs. Miller, also widowed; a 61-year-old scrublady, the sole support of her haggard old self. Got taken in a badly lit doorway on the 1500 block of Hyde Street. It's all written down in the morning Chronicle of that date. Well, possibly not *all*, but quite enough to make a careful eye blink. Blight read the article twice, then clipped it out for no good reason. And decided that it was someone's good luck that the Police so rarely read the crime stories they write. Not that Blight really cared one way or the other. And Mrs. Miller didn't care either. Perhaps she did care, once. But she has since learned that all is temporal in this accidental existence. And knowing this, she is at peace.

Arthritic old hag, with untidy, dirty gray hair and the odor of disinfectants, floor polish, and damp mops that followed her down Hyde Street at the fatal hour of 5:00 A.M. on a lawless Wednesday morning. . . .

. . . A garbage can, apparently overturned in the struggle, spilled its rank secrets over the mottle-faced drab—she, crumpled in a doorway, her skirt up around her hips. Her secrets also spilled.

But nobody seemed to notice. Nobody seemed the wiser. The spoor had been crossed, recrossed, and dipped thrice in trash. The bloodhounds chased their tails around in a circle, yapping and snapping at themselves in frustration. Their fathers, the Police assigned to the case, shook their fists at Heaven. And a few early morning thrill-seekers tried to get up close to the corpse. Alive, the lady wasn't worth the first glance, but tossed in a doorway, her naked legs made lewd by Death, more than one ogler found her absolutely fascinating.

Could she have been dancing, there at her demise? The

wild and abandoned sprawl of her limbs suggested that she had been taken at the apex of her leap; cut untimely in the moment of her tarantella. It seemed a shame to bury an old woman right in the middle of an orgasm, but it was probably better than not burying her at all. It was only good policy on the part of the Police to get the Dead buried as soon as they could. Else some smart somebody was going to notice the two neat bite marks on the throat of every woman who went to Glory on Wednesday morning. It wouldn't take long to put two and three together, and then all the newspapers in the city would be standing around on corners, asking pedestrians,

WHO DRINKS BLOOD IN FRISCO?

And the Police don't need any competition from a bunch of citizen vampire-hunters.

So they did to Mrs. Miller what they did to all the Wednesday victims. She was gone. Goodbye. And add another grudge to the growing file downtown at Central Headquarters. Where they held a Confidential Autopsy; after which they got rid of the body the way they always do. They know how.

So the deed was done with maximum security, and the Press was kept out, and some people began to wonder who was hiding what from whom?

How should Blight know?

And if Blight did know . . . how much did he know?

Why did they persecute him so terribly?

Why nuns, old scrubladies; why little girls, and bossy, middle-aged business women . . .?

Why do they wait until Monday to declare a red-headed corset shop owner, Missing Under Dubious Circumstances, when she was last seen Wednesday morning about ten o'clock, coming out of a competitor's shop, her arms full of bundles? This, on Market Street, according to the newspaper account. Approximately seventy-five meters from the employees entrance of the Travelers Hotel. Blight himself verified the distance, using a Brunswick tape measure. Of course five days had passed since the woman had stepped through this doorway, had left her competitor's shop for what, and where did she go? And did her way take her past the entrance used by employees of the Travelers? Used, to put it plainly, by none other than that overweighted, unsuspected, absentminded Nightclerk, who might forget a lot of things, but not his way around the catacombs that trickled off the employees entrance. Take that for what it's worth.

Don't bother to inspect Blight's lapels for red hairs, or wonder what he did with the body. Don't look for blood under his fingernails. Don't jump from innuendo to conclusion, and from there to consternation, alarm, and on to mindless panic, headlong flight, and unconsidered acts of phrenzy which will only bring about that which you most fear. . . . .

said Capt. O. R. Claw, Chief of the Vanished Ladies Dept. He told reporters that he was "apprehensive" over the rising number of ladies who were getting snatched out of the Frisco area. He promised a full-scale roundup of all known Offenders, Fiends, and Homoverts.

"We have their names and we intend to pull them in and to hold them tightly until we have found the man we're looking for." Claw said his plan had Community backing, and that his department was going ahead with retaliatory measures.

"We'll fight terror with terror," the Captain said in a

direct quote, but would neither confirm nor deny the rumor that a *quid pro quo* hostage system was under study by the Mayor and his son. "We will take whatever steps we feel are necessary," Claw

was covering up for Someone, with bombast, sensational interviews, drastic measures, and all the usual paraphernalia of an Official pacifying the public which was getting raped, murdered, disappeared, and only the victims know what else, every Wednesday morning in every single week.

Just how long did they think they could get away with it?

Wednesday morning again, and Mounted Police patrolling Golden Gate Park discover two girls hanging from a tree. Joanne Darling, 26, and Susan Grayfield, 22, were taken to County Hospital for treatment. . . .

. . . the Treatment was continued on the following Wednesday, in the basement of an all-night laundromat at 1149 Howell Street.

Mrs. Dee-Dee Hummer told Patrolmen Gawkins and Glub, who released the hog-tied, blindfolded, just redecorated housewife, early Wednesday morning in response to a note found by a milkman.

MONSTER MAKES IT AGAIN!

Dear Editor: I know that you will never have the nerve to print this letter but I am writing anyway to say that I have made a study of Social Misfits, chronic alcoholics, drug addicts, freqks, perverts, and so forth. And I have decided that these people should be destroyed. Painlessly of course. The normal citizens of this fair city have a right to be protected from this blight of abnormal freqks and parasites

Who may be found any morning but Wednesday morning, sunk in the gloomy Travelers lobby, sniffling, snuffing, wheezing, nodding, grunting, and sighing in what must not be mistaken for sleep, but must be respected as a state of magick: a trance into which Blight did withdraw at will, to hold converse with the dark and fearful Wonders whose Wednesday celebrations seemed somehow connected with a Nightclerk, wrapped in silence . . . patiently building his case in dreams. Collecting Wednesday morning newspapers and scissoring out the vital parts.

"I couldn't believe my eyes!" Gwaine Reynolds, 49, a part-time butler, told a Vigilante group investigating last Wednesday's pre-dawn doings at filmstar Bette Wunderlicht's Telegraph Hill penthouse.

"The man was wearing a Santa Claus disguise. My first thought was—what's a big, fat Santa Claus doing here in the middle of the night? Then Miss Wunderlicht, and Miss Gay, her Cosmetician, came running into my room scream-ing that they had been clip-pered, and sure enough, they had. They were both as bald as a baby's backside, and they hollered to me to stop the Santa."

Major Biteman, Vice-Chief of Vengeance, interrupted Reynolds' testimony at this point to ask if Reynolds, a former Karate instructor, had been able to get a good look at the attacker.

"I did my best, sir," the burly servant replied. "But he was too fast for me. It was like trying to stop a hippo with a butterfly net. He ran right through me, sir, and got clean away. Miss Wunderlicht knows how hard I tried. No, I didn't see his face. But I did see his Evil Eye."

"We have a detailed description of every evil eye in the State," Inspector C. C. Lillian, head of the Special Services & Nocturnal Traffic Bureau, reassured an 11th hour ad hoc committee that descended on City Hall yesterday afternoon to demand protection from Wednesday.

"My boys are working around the clock, and I can promise you that every suspicious looking man from here to Sacramento will be under lock and key before next Tuesday midnight."

Lillian's remarks drew cheers and sighs from Committee Officials, and were, of course, reprinted in the newspapers, where Blight read them. And then turned the page.

AUSTRALIAN SILKY TERRIERS. Gd.
with child. K. & K. Kennels. Watson-
ville.
GERMAN SHEPHERD. Male. Vicious.
Trn'd to p'tect women. $150. Mana-
scene Breeders. Longview. Clsd. Wed.
GAYTECKEL DACHSHUNDS. Standard,
smooth, also miniatures. Tp qual. Los
Lunas anyday aft. 5 p.m.

MISC. PETS

SMALL MONKEYETTE. Darling, clean,
loyal, gd. company. Warm eyes.
Nearly human. Pt. male. $10–$50.
Visit Pop's for all yr. pet needs.
PARROTS, BLACK CANARIES. Other
rare birds avail

a defenseless woman naught, when on an awful Wednesday dawning, she hears someone behind her. But before she can turn, before she can scream, a huge and puffy hand is clapped over her mouth, and her jaws are held tightly shut by fingers of steel.

OBEDIENCE TRAINING
Le Rue Grim. Every dog should be
trained. Private training and Group
classes

are being organized to teach women how to deal with sex maniacs and stranglers who seize girls from behind. At such a time, Marine murder instructors advised their female students, a hatpin, a pencil, or even a stiff forefinger can be a formidable weapon when jabbed into. . . .

. . . hundreds of dirty old men, as well as hundreds of unsavory younger men; shaggy fugitives, furtive fellows, have been registered and rearrested by Police in connection with the continuing Wednesday morning out-rages.

"It's an outrage!" Lieut. Ben Hacker of the Special Measures Squad denied charges of police brutality in questioning last Wednesday's suspects, nineteen of whom were seriously injured while falling down the steps, inside Central Headquarters. "Asking questions is only half our job," he said in a taped interview. "Getting answers is the other half. And we haven't time to coddle degenerates."

Mrs. Mary O'Tool, mother of one of the degenerates, was taken into custody when she tried to picket City Prison. Replying to criticism from Snivel Rights groups, Lieut. Hacker, visibly piqued, warned that further criticism was intolerable. "We will go on interrogating persons who might be able to tell us what we want to know until we have our man. We are going to talk to anybody who has anything whatsoever to do with Wednesday, and that's all there is to it. We're letting the O'Tool woman off blight."

But nobody came down to the Travelers Hotel to have a nice chat with Spenser. The only visitor from Central Headquarters was the regular Friday night bagman, making his regular tax and contribution collection. Nobody took the hint. The Police went their own way. The streetsweepers brushed away the threads that ran from Wednesday to Blight, the fat spider who sat spinning the night away in the rotten core of the haunted hotel. The hotel that floated, and drowned, and pulled up its windowshades, night after night, and exposed itself to the stragglers on Market Street. And never went out except on Tuesday night and Wednesday morning. . . . .
. . . . . . to get the newspapers, early edition, and find out what's been happening in the world. Sometimes a small shock gets through; for example when one reads that

> The blight from San Francisco was held for two hours while airport security men searched the plane. City police, acting on an anonymous tip, fingerprinted all passengers and

some printer's devil got a gold star for indifferent spelling.

But Central Obsession never caught on, and Blight continued to shift in the night, unaccused and unconfirmed. And occasionally pestered by cranks calling in just to let him know that he hadn't really been forgotten.

"Travelers Hotel. Good morning."

"Good morning, Spenser . . ."

"Hmmmmmmmmmmm?"

"I say there, Spenser, have you read the papers yet?"

"Not yet, no."

"Oh good. I wanted to be the first to tell you . . . there's the body of a woman, a Mary O'Doul, out near the college campus. She's been done to death, Spenser. And listen, the body's still warm! If you hurry . . ."

"See here you, *this isn't Wednesday!*"

A painful silence on the other end. "Oh," said the voice finally, "it isn't?"

"Click off," said Blight. "I'm busy now."

And so he was. So would any man be, sitting too close to a telephone switchboard at 4:00 A.M. Every time a new ghost walks, Spenser must listen to the same old threats, and promises, and garbled directions which would bring him to the scene of the crime, had he been fool enough to follow them.

J. Spenser Blight, as everyone knows, was a fat man who had no intention of going anywhere. He didn't have to: it all came to him. And it would come to any man; for the Living are the natural habitat of the Dead. Even though most people are too frightened to take in their own ghosts. Even though most people are among the first to blame, to point the black finger, to print slander in the newspapers, because every now and occasionally then, the greatest magickian might conceivably succumb to the evil they wouldn't accept, but turned loose in the night.

The chickens have come home to roost. That's why they hate Blight. Soon they'll be sorry and deeply ashamed.

V

Who, seeing the Nightclerk now, wheezing in his swivel chair, his mouth full of broken, black tusks, and his nostrils brass-plated from years of snuff taking . . . who can believe that this bald hippopotamus once tripped gaily the light fantastic, waltzing an Atlantic deck, as their ocean liner steamed toward Europe?

Katy in a bell-skirted ballgown, and Spenser in a dinner jacket of midnight blue. An extraordinarily attractive young couple making the Grand Tour.

Taking a trip.

Paris was disappointing. There were only five whores in the entire city. Five stale, bored old bags with stringy hair and dead white flesh, and those terrible glazed eyes that have stared too long. . . .

The people they met in Paris were all going to parties, and Spenser and Katy went along. In Paris, everyone went to parties to make love, and every bedroom closet held crowds of blasé peekers, who had seen it all ages ago.

Neither Spenser nor Katy could recall having visited the City of Light before, but nearly everyone seemed to recognize them. They stayed only long enough for Katy to appear in a film, and then they traveled on to less exhausted regions. (This cineventure, henceforth to be known as Katy's Folly, will be elaborated upon in pages to come.

"Dove vai, cappuccetto Rosso?"	**Where are you going, little Red Riding Hood?**
"Cuanta questa, la cositita?"	**How much costs the little thing?**

96

"Putaine partout et cocus partout un Chastete n' habite pasenune region plus qu'en l'autre."

"Whores everywhere and cuckolds everywhere. Chastity dwells in one region no more than in another . . ."

"It is truly said, Monsieur," an unctuous shopkeeper of Karyes, the most celebrated servant mart on the Aegean Peninsula, fawned at Spenser's passing remark, and caught at his sleeve.

"Whips, harnesses, feathers, something pretty for your lady?" He looked at Katy and licked his lips. Katy looked back and licked hers. The merchant blanched; he'd never seen a purple tongue, and he knew nothing about vascular control. He was a hard-working marketman and how should he know parlor tricks from appearances? He sank to his knees between the stalls. "Forgive me, mad mother," he said very simply. "I did not know that I was in a Presence. Your mercy, White Queen."

"I do give it," signed Katy, most graciously inclining her head. "Rise up now and do as I bid."

"Gladly," said the mongoose; only a Tradesman, but not of mean imagination. A devout man, and not less astute, he always said the appropriate prayer; he always made a sale. "Only say what you would have of me."

"Something that white men never see," Spenser spoke for Katy. "Take us to the inner market. We would look on the Bench of ZaG'ob."

Again the Caftan bowed. "It will be difficult to arrange, but it shall be done. Only I must pray you not to bring your cameras. It is forbidden," he added with a reverent flash of his teeth.

And that very afternoon they were taken, in mufti, to a coffee house deep in the native quarter, and there they saw the fabled Bench designed by the dissipated Morovian Emperor, Nickoli ZaG'ob. . . . The obscene board fitted out with thirty-three pegs, cunningly carved from flesh-tinted peachwood, varying in thickness and length, and so spaced that thirty-three pleasure boys at a time could seat themselves upon the pegs and there wait on the wealthy voluptuaries, the oily sheiks up from Persia, and degenerate fig farmers flown in from Syria, and an occasional Turk to make the boys tremble . . . and now Blight and wife come to salute ingenuity, to watch the pederasts make their choice by lifting up a likely lad and noting the size of peg he was perched on.

By sunset all of Karyes had heard and was scandalized, and a three-hundred-year-old tradition was terminated when Katy, quick as a cat, left her table to take a recently vacated place on the Bench.

A few days later, on the Isle of Trifler, they only just escaped another incident. They had not been informed of the local custom, which encouraged the bravos, the fierce men of that obscure and very ancient island, to wear the prettiest girls they could catch, like plumes stuck in their enormous, woolly headgear.

A sympathetic North African smuggler got them away for a staggering sum of gold, and Katy's company in his cabin.

That the latter requirement was fulfilled, we may be certain of, but since the bold smuggler's body has never been found, we may only guess at the currency in which he was paid.

Meanwhile Blight and Katy traveled into Egypt, there to partake of unusual excesses.

They saw vile things done along the Nile. They ate *meryet*, the Hemaken aphrodisiac prepared from the scrapings of a crocodile's penis. This potion of passion was so potent that Katy's highly susceptible senses were overstimulated to such an extent that it was necessary to bury her up to her neck in soft, wet mud; and, so constrained, she was subjected to oral indecencies by her husband, their two guides, and a score of camel-drivers, part of a caravan providentially passing by just when their services were most appreciated. But even with such energetic assistance, many hours took their time with Katy, before Spenser deemed her reason returned.

Then he dug her up, distributed token coins and amulets among the rough men who had cooled Katy's ardor, and they drove back through the desert dawn, reaching their hotel in Cairo just before noon.

About ten hours later, still in Cairo, Katy complained of an awful headache. A physician who'd trained in London comforted her with a handful of morphine; X-rayed her skull and located the pain in the general region of the external carotid artery. His official diagnosis was cephalalgia, or, a pain in the head. Privately, he suggested Possession. It was entirely possible, Spenser very well knew.

They stayed until the morphine was gone, then flew back to Europe, and following the dying words of their Egyptian physician, Katy entered the most expensive sanatorium in Switzerland.

The headaches were occurring with obstinate regularity despite the best beards and most solemn stethoscopes that money could buy. Then Spenser, in desperation, asked help from his magick, and the answer came back singing in the wind.

When other treatments fail, good deeds often serve.

. . . Now

Blight had long cherished the desire to make love to a woman in the throes of a *grand mal* seizure, and t'was Katy, acting on spirit council, who made his indecent dream come true. It was she who had made the costly arrangements that closeted Spenser with Monique, a young Danish epileptic. And it was

Katy who corrupted Monique's nurse, Katy who stole the stroboscope, the flickering light that put Monique in the mood. Without her even knowing it.

She came awake to a flicker that artfully triggered her psychomotor reflexes. Between Blight and her convulsions she never knew what hit her. Days later, she recalled the attack as particularly severe. And her nurse quite agreed, with an involuntary tremor. She had been well paid, but it still hurt like hell. . . . Blight rising from the wrung-out Monique, his central inhibitions removed by the intensity of stimulus, Blight was in a state of extraordinary sensual fusion. Monique, unconscious on her stomach, one arm dangling over the edge of the bed. Blight swayed on his feet and the nurse, victim of her training, stepped forward. Blight fell on her, and the sexual-clasp reflex took care of the rest. He had her by the light of the blinking strobe. Then held her while Katy. And so forth.

The monsters . . . !

"Yes, dear. It was a *very* violent attack. I nearly ruptured myself trying to hold you."

Those two . . . what were they trying to do?

"How's your headache, darling?" Spenser asked, as the taxi took them away from the sanatorium and to the railroad station.

"O it's wonderful, Spenser. It's just wonderful."

The above incident is remarked upon mainly to fix the *primo* appearance of those excruciating headaches that cursed Katy from time to torturous time.

Unfortunately, we may not be so precise in regard to that initial manifestation of תיבל : *Bar Habor*, as it is given in the Solomonic Lemegaton, or *Bar Habvor*, according to Precfret's revised *Pseudomonarchia Daemonorum*.

Bar Habvor, that obscure and lonely Hebraic demon whose province it is to haunt the dismal rooftops on windy nights, hoping to overhear some snatch of forbidden conversation between husband and wife, or better, between father and daughter. (In Katy's case, of course, he came too late for the latter, and was forever pestering her to tell him tales from her childhood.)

As may be readily imagined, their relationship was symbiotic, though Bar Habvor's origins were vague, and inspired much conjecture. On winter evenings, snug around a crackling fire, in an Austrian ski lodge, Katy and Spenser played chess, worked crossword puzzles, and tried to guess where their devil came from. . . .

Spenser recalled a certain curious chap, the Assistant Curator of the Ibex Collection, the private library at the Institut für Sexualwissenschaft, in Munich. But for the very kind and helpful services of the small, humpbacked, damp-eyed Assistant, they would certainly have overlooked some of the choicest items. Why had the man—if he were a man—been so attendant upon them? And why, after they were done at the library, had the good fellow continued to wait upon them? Were his motives other than carnal when he took them to that exclusive nightclub, just outside the city limits, where they ate food named for Jewish children, and applauded a floorshow which featured a wrestling match between a strapping milkmaid and a dwarf?

Very droll.

And after the floorshow, the Blood Rites.

"That's where we got him," Spenser said. "Remember, I thought it was gangrene at first. And the pharmacist in Düsseldorf thought it was jungle rot. . ."

"Nonsense," Katy maintained. She offered that Bar Habvor had erupted, fully clothed, from a pustule acquired in the Egyptian misadventures with camel-boys, with Arabs lured from their casbahs, with petty sheiks, and movie actors enroute to cineasia. It was a wonder that she'd only caught the measles.

And it would have been much worse if massive dosages of anti-biotics and methedrine had not miraculously blighted the fruits of her evil. Katy reasoned that according to the 3rd Law of Retribution, such a harvest could not be *entirely* averted. And Bar Habvor was the result: a sort of unnatural agreement twixt science and the traditions of guilt . . . "Really, Spenser, isn't it obvious?"

"Perhaps, perhaps," Spenser mumbled, not much inclined to argue details. The orange flames danced on the left side of his face. For all he knew, Bar Habvor might very well be the embodiment of a complicated curse that a bearded lady, billed as Mademoiselle Hairee, had hurled at them one sultry evening the previous summer, when, on the outskirts of Budafok, he and Katy had commissioned a very private performance of a specialized circus. . . . No. Spenser had no desire to debate political or religious problems.

He didn't blame the kind Assistant Curator for Germany's Crime, and neither had he any inclination to find fault with Katy for forgetting where she'd picked up their demon.

As for Katy, she agreed in principle, and also refrained from pressing the point. Spenser might suspect whomsoever he pleased, but she would continue to keep her personal opinions warm and dry.

In Bar Habvor, she perceived some quality very reminiscent of their sojourn in India, and their visit to the temple near Srirangam, where the *gopuras* were decorated with not less than thirty thousand figurines and statuettes, and every single one of them engaged in copulatory activities. Every beautiful, obscene and graven image in that fabulous temple, only a few hours from Rapipur, home of elephantine eroticism, anticipated Katy and Spenser.

All morning they'd wandered about, delighting in the indecent artistry; and then the blazing noontime caught them without their hats . . . Katy still considered fainting when she recalled the terrible sun that had sent them reeling through the gardens of Agapusha, that incredible Goddess, who, on account of her own deformities, takes the most intense pleasure in bizarre exhibitions. . . .

Behind the crumbling walls of Her sanctuary lay the desolate and heart-rending plains of Boas. So difficult to believe that only a few centuries ago, the gold and teakwood Shrine of Ishnu had extended from the temple to the Rapipuran suburbs, and had a permanent population of some nine thousand *veśya, ganikā,* first-grade courtesans, and staff prostitutes. And of all this, all that remained were the scrubby rocks and scabby underbrush; a few small, quick, and very frightened, scaly creatures; some black boulders, widely spaced; here and there a pillar of salt, and a sandy wasteland in between.

Within the Pavilion of Agapusha, no one worshiped at the Sacred Lingam. No crowds of pilgrims performed the Congress of Crows, or observed the ancient Tantric courtesies. Not a single *dhoti* could be seen anywhere in the main *sikhara*.

Only foreigners or mad dogs would be fools enough to be about at such a merciless hour. The midday sun was out to murder. They sought shade under the slender arches of the myriad *mithunas,* and there, gasping, blinking, swooning, they were found by the temple custodian and Bangalī monk, Jaya-dera. A man of magnificent proportions, nearly seven feet tall, the color of mahogany, his black hair shot through with streaks of silver; he smiled at Spenser and offered the comforts of the Black Pavilion.

"It is forbidden to bring the uninitiated there," his smile grew even wider. "But you two are different. If you will please to follow me . . ."

And in the monk's company they entered the most holy lingarāj, where they did linger till the molten afternoon had purpled to dusk, and the phallic shadows stretched out across the sun-blasted temple yard. An ox lowed in the distance, and the demon-haunted Indian night came rushing down upon them.

It was at some time during that pagan afternoon—Katy was almost positive—that Bar Habvor had attached his self to her. And Katy had a damned good idea at *exactly* what time, and in what spot, that infernal entrance had been effected.

At the edge of the divine pavilion, just off the path that led to the Caves of Mysore, a darkened, passionate niche, carved from limestone, the floor covered with peacock feathers . . . such a cleverly designed cul-de-sac. Katy never saw it until she was in it, with the monk, Jayadera. Spenser, completely engrossed in the *damputi* friezes and the famous (O justifiably so!) murals of Mythe Outcaste Women, the Tantric cult of female deviationists; he wandered on, apparently oblivious of Katy's absence.

She, of course, had not the opportunity to cry out, or make the slightest sound to gain his attention. The Monk's right hand covered her mouth, and for an instant Katy was amused at the fellow's unnecessary precautions. But the next instant, his left hand did something so unbelievably crude that she *certainly would have screamed* if the tall, handsome, horribly cruel custodian had not held her so tightly; silenced her so effectively.

And he kept doing it to her until he'd charmed and humiliated her spirit by a device described in the *Rig Veda,* and popularly known as the Six Syllables. Not until she undid her heart in front of him, and in front of whoever else was in that alcove with them; not until he was satisfied that she had felt the *Vaja,* the Thunderbolt of Shiva, did he release her, stuttering and full of confusion, all blushes and tingles, to stumble out into the daylight, after Spenser who had disappeared into the cave of worship, where she found him in rapt contemplation, on his knees before the terra cotta plaque which idealized a triad, two Palace slaves and a fat King, *in coitu.*

"Most magnificent example of the pre-Vedic art that I've ever seen!" Spenser exclaimed reverently, as Katy rushed up to him. The monk, Jayadera, had not yet joined them; and before Katy could tell him what had happened to her, Blight sprang with the speed and finesse of a master thief. (Who doubts it?) With a thin, Oslo-forged blade, he pried the plaque from the wall and pushed it into Katy's hands.

"What . . . ?"

"Quick! Hide it under your skirt!" He whipped out his belt and, never hesitating, strapped the treasure twixt her legs and flat against her abdomen. The whole affair, from snatch to snatch, had not taken fifteen seconds.

"Our friend, the careless custodian, isn't likely to go between your thighs so soon after he's just been there." Spenser saved her honor, and got for them a masterpiece. And Katy, when she realized it, was far too grateful to mar the moment with further complications. She took his arm, and moving like a Fairie Dame, so as not to reveal the outlines of the plaque beneath her skirt, she accompanied him out of the caves just as Jayadera emerged from the nookorium: nearly eighty-four inches of flashing smile and dark, heroic disinterest. He had given the Christian female what her theologians (he projected) would term, *the Devil's caresse.* This Hindu ravisher, this handsome, toothy, dharma bigot, loved, above and beyond his vows, to pluck the jewel from the baptized lotus. And on this occasion, he had thought himself eminently successful.

And Blight, he thought, an atrociously cuckolded tourist. But he changed his mind when, months later, the plaque was discovered missing. The Courts of Maitreya, the future Buddha, assumed that Jayadera had stolen it, and had him tortured most exquisitely to death. . . . And his last thoughts were on Blight and Katy.

He died gnashing his teeth.

While the two objects of his ultimate reflections, Spenser and spouse Katy, were already ten thousand miles away, and still in swift transit.

And for all their triumph, Katy had to admit—to herself, if to no one else—that, rude as the Monk had been, never before had she been so thoroughly debauched by a single stroke.

Spenser, her lover and her champion, might assume whatever he damn well chose to assume. Theory is always inferior to sensation, and Katy had, after all, *felt* Bar Habvor leap into her bosom as the Monk's device drove home . . . !

". . . Oh, don't be silly," said Spenser, pulling the bellcord that would summon the ski lodge maid for to throw another log on the fire. He turned back to Katy, chiding her gently. "You have the most unreasonable imagination, my dear. Absolutely no conception of geography! Really m'love, what do you suppose a Semitic devil like ours would be doing in an Indian monastery?"

Katy raised her penciled eyebrows and answered in the sweetest voice, "What were we doing there?"

And Spenser was still trying to think of an answer, five minutes later, when the perfect servant, her red hair piled atop her head, and her uniform unbuttoned to the waist, tapped respectfully at their door.

"Monsieur wishes me for burning?" she inquired in charming, literal English.

And that was how it went, each time they tried to remember where . . . they forgot more. Each time they played guessing games, they left the origins of this wicked Familiar further and further behind them. But the imp, himself, they eluded never. Where they went, he went with them. And his many, many guises, his most excellent disguises, were a source of constant wonder, and his skill at tempting them in tones seductive and suggestively succulent, turned Spenser olive-green with envy.

And though he told them a secret or two, never did he tell them where he came from. Neither would he tell them where they were all going. . . .

. . . or why poor Katy's head would suddenly begin to throb, and a pinkish fluid run out of her eyes, and invisible, white-hot needles (some of them almost twelve inches long!) were inserted into her quivering, aristocratic nostrils. Then she would taste cobalt in her mouth. . . . Of all the miserly understatements in all the inadequate dialects of men, surely *headache* is the puniest and most oversimplified of the so-called descriptive nouns. As if a *headache* of Katy's simply made her head to ache!

Was it only an ache then that caused the wisps of smoke that trickled out of her ears and rose over her head, there to hang in sympathetic clouds?

While she screamed and wept and rocked back and forth as waves of pain washed over her, rolled back, and washed in again; receding only long enough to give her time to howl before the next tide smashed through her. Agony that rippled as it rolled, and made her tongue to bleed, her nipples to crack, her fingernails to turn purple, and her suffering toes to curl.

While she groaned and panted, and was soon reduced to piteous prayers, which—Bar Habvor had warned her in no uncertain terms—could only hope to succeed if they were delivered in the most abject and groveling fashion. . . . Down on her knees! Lick the floor! Climb walls! Say Uncle! Say it! Louder! Funnier!

O he had his merry moments with her before he condescended to take notice of her pain and her urgent, tearful supplications. He was of such implacable cruelty, her Bar Habvor. Katy found herself depending upon it, more and more.

He hurt her dreadfully. But he never disappointed her.

And Spenser, always eager to learn new tricks, kept a careful vigil.

VI

But even Blight must sometimes sleep, or so he believed in those dim days . . . before he'd discovered how much a nap could cost.

Unscrupulous persons connected with the motion picture industry had tricked Katy out of her signature. Without Spenser's knowledge, of course, they'd buttered her vanity, projected her ego onto a shallow silver screen, and made her to sign away her gold, all for to be in the movies-O . . . !

". . . Oh! You stupid bitch! You stupid, stupid . . . ! You . . . !" foamed Spenser, not without some reason, when he'd found out what she had done. Found out, via a cable from their bank in New York to the private yacht they'd rented; all the better to cruise the gay Mediterranean waters.

Torpedoed off the coast of Sardina.

"Sir!"

the First Mate saluted smartly. "This message was just received."

He handed Spenser a gold-braided envelope, saluted again. "Will there be an answer, sir?"

"Stand at ease, First Mate McDuff." Katy loved to put the crew through close-order drill.

"Oh! You stupid bitch! You . . . !"

"Is something wrong, Spenser?"

The paper fluttered from Blight's fingers. The First Mate bent and retrieved the cablegram from the deck and handed it to Katy. Then he betook himself prudently and immediately to another part of the ship. He was an officer and a sensible gentleman, and when Blight's face began to turn black, he realized that he was needed elsewhere.

"Read it . . ." Spenser hissed, and Katy blinked.

109

LK24 MARINE MESSAGE 13 PD INTL FM BANK
TP BLIGHTS C/O YACHT VIA RCA MEDTRADIO
RANT:
    BE ADVISED YOU HAVE NO MORE MONEY.
    YR. INVES. AMERICAN BEAUTY STUDIOS,
    LTD. HAS RUINED YOU.

"What investment?" Spenser's voice made the wind die. Their sails shriveled, and their ship hung over the suddenly becalmed future. "What investment? I made no investment. Katy, *did you* make an investment?"

We need not wait for her answer, nor stay for the detailed explanation. Enough to say that she did, that she had signed on the dotted line, somewhere in Paris, on location. Which damn well taught Spenser a lesson. Too late. Too bad.

The crew wept. The Captain threatened to shoot the First Mate. The Italian Government apologized profusely. But t'was all to no avail. They had to pack and leave at once for California, where the defunct studio was located. This, a desperate attempt to salvage something.

Then, with no little regret, it was Goodbye, Goodbye. . . . *Farewell to the stinking lace and the ratty fur pieces; the beslobbered leather boots, belts, harnesses, and whips of Europe. That old whorehouse so filthy rich in historical drama . . . Europe, the torture chamber from whence our forefathers fled* (and which Blight and Katy had revisited). *The old gruesomes . . . the old sources . . . the old manacles and Bastille belts; the old and wormy, spine-stretching screamracks; the venerable Spanish mouth-gag, that time-honored agony pear, to spread the jaws, to stifle the scream. . . .*

So recite the opening lines, Canto I, of "L'Apo-pemptic d'Orly," penned at the airport of that name, while the Blights waited for the flight, already regretting Europe, lost. . . .

Europe and its great, and ancient artifacts. The jongs and belly chain, the crotch strap, and the iron boot, the spiked collar, the strappadoes, and the basti-nadoes. In Europe they do those things so well. . . . Now must we leave the cork-lined boudoir where the Scavenger's Daughter bit us goodbye. As we went out from the custody of the Iron Warden, and the beaded lampshade waved Goodbye, Goodbye to those dun-geons. . . .

Here.

This packet of picture postcards. Filthy-O! Photo-graphs of famous ghosts, in poses reproduced too often. . . .

. . . cobblestones covered with moss, dung, blood, and spilt wine of antiquity. The poules lining both sides of this street; striking classic poses under classic lamplight flickering. . . . Whores hissing from the doorways. Whores leaning out of ground-floor windows, their breasts bared; they moo and oink at the promenaders and boulevardiers.

Such restless whores, passing, pacing, strolling up and down the sidewalks of le Rue Grim, le Calle de Los Sueños Barbarosos, der Piffenstrasse. The staccato of their crippling, six-inch highheels, passing up and down on the sidewalks. Machine guns firing in the night cities of Europa.

Then, goodbye your goodbyes, you overcultivated continent. Goodbye your graveyards, your museums, your thousands of streets walked by your vast armies of venal women . . . a Venus for every mood, every idiom. Katy's prototypes.

Venus Peribasin and Venus Mucheia, Venus Castnia, and Venus Scotia, Venus Derceto, Venus Carte Blanche . . . the Straddling Venus, Venus of the Hetaira, the Venus who protects the girls of the cafés, the sidewalks, the *maisons de plaisir* . . . a Venus who loves nuns and women in prisons. A Venus of Indecent Copulations, and her sister, Venus Callipygo: the Corrupting Venus, Venus of Lairs and Retreats. Venus of the beautiful buttocks. . . .

". . . Baby Lulu, Sonya Sonic, Terry Gale, Gerry Tail, Gee-Gee Whiz, Frisky Lane, Karen Klaus, Dolly Big, Daisy Bell, Lucki Phele, and this new kid, she's just sensational, that's all. Sensational. We were going to call her, Oddette Lollypop. How do you like that for a marquee name? Not that it matters anymore. Goddamn shame that we never had a chance to use her," sighed the nearly bald, heavily sun-tanned head of the bankrupt studio. "I had her slated for a slot in our very next film. Unfortunately, there isn't going to be a next film."

His two major stockholders, Katy and Spenser, eyed him bleakly. The Promoter, crouched behind his smile, fingered his earlobe, and looked out of the office window. Hollywood Boulevard rolled below him. Bland, blue skies overhead.

"Kids, with the best intentions in the world, there just isn't anything I can do. We're broke, and that's it." A good promoter is a practicing philosopher. "Mr. Blight, I can only say how very sorry I . . ."

Bunko-men who insist upon staring their dupes right in the eye should know that they can get into serious trouble by staring too deeply. Not every dupe is as dumb as the dupe before him, nor as defenseless as he might seem. There are certain dupes with whirlpools in their eyes, and all sorts of magick in their voices.

"Mr. Blight, I can only . . . I can only . . . only . . ."

"Yes," Blight murmured. "*Keep staring into my eyes.*"

Katy sat very still, humming the Hypnotica Profundus.

"*Keep staring.*" Blight burned through the Promoter. "*You will do as I order you.*"

"Yes . . ."

"Give me your wallet."

"Yes . . ."

Blight set a pocket-sized metronome on the desk. "Watch that for a while," Blight told the Promoter, turning his own attention to the wallet. No cash, but lots of papers.

Mesmer himself couldn't get blood from a nugget of California fool's gold. The best Blight could wring from that wallet full of beautifully engraved *cartes de crédit* was a flimsy pink slip of paper that proved that the Promoter owned an automobile.

Mr.

"Sign here." Mrs. . . . .

Miss

Blight twisted the man's soul, made him to put his mark on a line not less dotted than the one that Katy had been tripped up on. "Take advantage of my nymphomaniac, will you?" Blight muttered, blotting the other's signature. Then, giving the Promoter a final command, and implanting a deep and destructive suggestion that caused the Promoter to stutter from that moment on until the day of his death, the Blights took their Consolation Prize, the Promoter's Mercedes convertible, and drove north.

First, Katy wanted to put the top down. Then she wanted to know where they were going.

"Where . . . ? Why, we're going into business, dear.

That's where." Blight swung the car onto the Great Highway. "Oh . . . that's fun." Katy smiled vaguely and said no more. Spenser had taught her to love a mystery.

One week later, from the second story of an apartment in San Francisco, overlooking a highschool yard, Blight and another man watched a softball game through two pair of high-powered binoculars. The rotund gent beside Blight, a short, easily winded puffball of sixty-six crime-crusted years, licked his puffy lips with the flat, dove-gray tongue of the true connoisseur. A quartette of trim youngsters, barelegged, passed out of the schoolyard carrying their books. Doctor Grabow followed them with his field glasses . . . saucy little rumps twitching, their short, plaid skirts hiking up in back as they went by. Charming as colts. Awkwardly tottering along on unaccustomed highheels.

"A mite early, those four," wheezed the good Doctor, when they were out of sight. He lowered his spyglasses and rubbed his red-rimmed eyes. "I try to be here every afternoon at three o'clock, especially Fridays. Yes Fridays, that's the best day, you know. The sweeties are so sprightly on Friday. That's when they wear all their prettiest do-jiggers, and sometimes the older girls, the Seniors, they might be wearing a smidgeon of lipstick, or maybe little bitty highheels. That's why I like Fridays the best. If you take my meaning . . ."

". . . 'deed I do, Doctor, 'deed I do," Spenser purred nastily. He was watching the girls' softball team finishing their game in one corner of the yard. The window was above and behind home plate, affording a delightful view of a pigtailed catcher's tender crotch. Mostly for Dr. Grabow's benefit, Blight sighed.

"See something special?" the Doctor was always overeager. He snatched up his binoculars again.

Two Bird-watchers, risking eyestrain for the opportunity of studying the adolescent, twittering flocks of highschool chippies. The three o'clock buzzer set them free.

The Doctor was beside himself as they poured through the gate. "Oh, yes indeedy-do, little Missy!" Dr. Grabow occasionally spoke in tongues. Especially when the occasion included thirteen, fourteen, and even fifteen year olds.

Stampeded children made his old heart thump so hard it hurt. But he couldn't stop. Not now. Not with hundreds of them pouring through the open gate.

"Look at that one! That one over there! The darling chubby over there! Oh! Those two! Oh look! Oh . . . !"

Blight feared for the old boy's thumping, bumping, over-stimulated heart. Fortunately, the rush of kids ended at last, and only a few stragglers appeared, crossed the yard, and disappeared up the street. By 3:30 the school seemed empty.

"Quite a workout, that." Dr. Grabow reluctantly lowered his glasses. "Oh dear, another day . . . ended." Old Doc's voice quivered with pity for poor old Doc; pudgy, sixty-six-year-old Doc, who lived alone in an apartment across from the highschool. He began to whine. "All week long I look forward to Fridays. Then on Friday, I can't wait till Monday. The weekends are so empty, don't you know. The children aren't in school . . ."

Blight stuck to his glasses, although no one but a fat spinster schoolteacher—he knew she was a spinster from the way she walked—had left the school since 3:45. "Hmmmmm. Yes. Of course. That's the absolute truth. Pity. No school on the weekends, you say . . . and the little tarts off in the bushes, I'll wager."

Dr. Grabow tittered. "My goodness, Blight, but you have the most puerile imagination . . ."

"By my mother!" Blight suddenly exclaimed, hunching forward. "Could that possibly be who I think it is?"

"Who? Where? Which way . . . ? For Christ's own sake, where . . . !" the Doctor snatched up his glasses.

"That girl, crossing the yard . . . *I know her!*"

The two men watched the solitary figure, a slim girleen, prescribed schoolbooks in her arms, she glided across the deserted yard. Four o'clock shadows licked at her legs . . . her long, absolutely stunning legs.

"Oh, my precious monkey glands," the Doctor marveled, and hiccuped happily. "I can hardly believe it. I ask you, have you ever seen such extraordinarily long legs on such a young filly? In all my years . . . all the teenflesh that I've looked at, I swear I can't recall ever seeing such a wonderfully leggy little creature. And you say you know her? Is that what you said, Blight? You actually know her? My gracious Oh! How altogether too perfectly delightsome for you, dear Blight. How lucky. How . . ." the Doctor lowered his glasses long enough to peek at Blight . . . "*How well* do you know her, if I may ask?"

Blight winked. Dr. Grabow shivered. He went back to staring at the girl.

He'd guess her to be about fifteen. Tall for her age, but Grabow had seen enough teeners to know that some were taller than others. . . . And even if she was all of sixteen years old . . . *sixteen!*

A bright red ribbon held the girl's long, pitch-black hair away from her fragile, porcelain, doll-like forehead. She hugged her books to her chest, so that the Doctor was denied an opportunity to fairly estimate her mammary development. Still, from the shape of her shoulders and the already pronounced curve of her hips, he'd guess that the fruit was just ripe and ready for plucking beneath her sap-green sweater.

Dr. Grabow almost dropped his binoculars. The little charmer! She'd caught her sandal heel in a sidewalk grating, and for a teasing, teetering, highwire second, her plaid skirt flew up as she struggled to keep her balance. She came very close to tipping over, but saved herself just in the nick. By a quick. And a hop, skip, and she was out of the trap. . . .

. . . Doctor Grabow breathed again. He watched her hobble back to the yard. Watched her as she leaned against the wire fence and took off her shoe, inspecting for possible damage to the heel. Grabow fiddled with the fine-adjustment knob, increased his magnification. Inspecting her inspecting, so to speak. . . .

"How well do you know her, Blight? Who does she belong to? Who . . . ?"

"Easy at it, Doctor." Blight would hate to lose the old man now, by some ironic stroke or attack. "Hold yourself calm, my dear Doctor. *Calm* . . . it is the only way, I assure you."

"But who . . . ? How . . . ?"

"How do I know her? She's the daughter of a friend of a friend. Grabow, good chap, now will you be calm!"

The Doctor swallowed a small white pill. He breathed deeply. He took hold of himself. He smiled without mirth to show that he was his old self once again. "Must forgive me, Blight. My apologies. Friday afternoon, you know. Get carried away." He lifted the binoculars and

On with the Show!

The exceptionally juicy child was still standing on one leg, swaying somewhat. The Doctor plucked at a knob on his instrument, twisting it a centimeter this way, half a centimeter that way, all the better to see the sweet curve of thigh. . . .

"Now then, Blight. You were saying . . . ?"

"She's the daughter of someone . . . shall we say, *someone who may be reached.*"

"Ah. And may I ask how old she is? What's her name? And . . ." the Doctor was getting excited again.

Blight's tones were calculatedly soporific, a lullaby voice to rock the big baby's cradle. "Fifteen, going on sixteen, Doctor. And her name is Cay . . ."

"Exactly as I'd supposed." The Doctor kept the binoculars to his straining eyes. "Nearly sweet sixteen . . . how I do wonder, has she ever been kissed?" Grabow, of course, was talking to himself. But Blight overheard.

". . . kissed her alright. Had no choice, you understand. As it happened, I was staying overnight at her father's home. Parents divorced, naturally. Child's literally starving for affection. Crawled right into my bed, she did. And her father and stepmother sleeping in the next room. Will you look at her . . . that innocent, tender, not-quite-sixteen-year-old child . . . whispered to me that she'd not leave until I would . . . but of course I wouldn't. Couldn't, you know. But I did . . . and she loved it. *I say, please be easy there, Doctor!* Why don't you unbutton your shirt collar . . . breathe a bit easier, hey?"

"Then what happened? Blight, I must know!"

"Why, certainly you must know, Doctor Grabow. If I had suspected that you might be interested . . . you are *interested?* Yes, of course you are. I say, Doctor, I think that I might just possibly be of some small service to you."

Grabow bit his lip. It was painful to hope . . . "Ah my sweet Blight, my fine friend, you wouldn't torture an old man?"

Blight shrugged. He yawned. "If I were going to torture anyone, it wouldn't be an old man. No offense, but old men just don't do a thing for me."

"What I mean, did I understand you correctly? That is, you did say that you could arrange . . ."

"I said *perhaps*, now Grabow. I said *perhaps*. But it is within reasonable conjecture. You see, since that quasi-consummated night, I have, by the queerest bit of excellent fortune, come into . . . some information. Certain information that puts the pretty child's father entirely within my power. Or to put it another way . . . he'll do exactly what I tell him to."

"But his own daughter? Are you sure?"

"The man we are discussing is completely without scruples. In return for my information—unless I sadly misjudge my man—he'll turn his daughter over to me and consider himself let off cheaply. You see . . ."

". . . see! Ha! See that!" Grabow ejaculated. "Did you see that! She fell from Grace, she did!"

Blight lifted his glasses. The Doctor was right. Still on one leg, the child had tried to put her shoe back on, but her balance was tipped, and she slipped,

and over she went. Whoops . . . !

After her cunning acrobatics on the sidewalk grate, Katy took an unrehearsed pratfall. And her skirts flew up around her waist.

"Whee!" whinnied the old Grabow goat. "Did you see? She don't wear no underwear!"

Thanks to the expensive binoculars, Blight saw very well. He saw Katy's face turn red. But by no sign, or side-glance, did she betray what she very well knew. Not once did she look up at the second-floor window across the street. But she was blushing all the same.

In a hurry now, she found her feet, tugged her skirt down, and hurried off, up the street. Hobbled, actually. One shoe on and one shoe off. . . .

". . . diddle-diddle dumpling. You bet your anything that I'm interested. How soon . . . ?"

"There you go again, Doctor. First questions first. Not how soon, until we have settled, *how much?*" Blight put the binoculars away and moved closer to the bloody-eyed, guppy-mouthed, old rumpled tub of illegal desire. "Now listen to me. Grabow . . ."

"How much . . . ?" Grabow repeated piteously. "Oh, how much . . ."

"But even that question is premature. The first thing we must know is . . . *what?*

"What?"

"Yes, *what.* What do you intend to do with her? What do you want her for? Don't be embarrassed. But you must tell me everything . . ."

Blight leaned closer. The old man talked. Slowly, reluctantly at first, then more readily, until finally the tale was spinning out as fast as he could mouth it.

Blight listened most intently. He realized that it was only a first draft. Grabow would improve, would tighten the dream, and print up stage directions, cue sheets. Eventually they'd have a complete shooting script. Blight never doubted it. For the time being, however, he would settle for a rough idea, a general outline. And when he got it, he cut the Doctor off with an urgent tweak of his earlobe.

"Hear me, Doctor . . ." And Blight told the fellow his dream right back to him; told him in the most sibilant of whispers.

"I could do that much for you," Blight concluded. "And then I'd leave the room and you could . . ."

". . . Oh, but that's just exactly what I want so much to do!"

"Do as I say then, and you shall have . . ." said Blight.

"You are a thoroughly monstrous fellow, Blight! I think that you must be insane. No offense, dear man, no offense. I mean . . . are you certain that there'd be no risk?"

"No risk." Blight swore. "A Safe-conduct Pass is included in the price."

"The price . . . ?"

"Exactly," said Blight. "We have now reached the point of *how much?*"

"I'm not a rich man," Doctor Grabow went down on his knees. "But you must get me that girlie."

Blight patted the supplicant's trembling shoulder. "There-'re a few little things that you must get me," he explained. "Now a skilled apothecary and a physician (Ret.) of your skill with a Narcotics License—I assume that you still retain your Federal Permit? Ah yes, very wise of you. And I dare say that you might even find a pharmaceutical orderblank or two, if you really started looking . . ."

"To be sure . . . to be sure." Hope, and the first glimmer of comprehension crept into the Doctor's liver-spotted face. "You want some . . ."

"Na-Na!" said Blight sharply. "Let's not call a rose by its first name. These are perilous times, Doctor. Never forget it. And the walls are quite capable of selling our best secrets if we should be so careless as to sing them out audibly. Caution . . . always caution! I cannot impress that upon you too strongly . . . now fetch me your pharmacopoeia. There are some brand names I want to look up. And some paper, if you please. I'll give you a list of the necessary ingredients. Then we'll have our minds nice and free and all ready to think about you and the undisciplined child . . ."

"Ah . . . Oh."

"My sentiments exactly, Doctor. Most fortunate that you should happen along at such a moment. I can tell you that the child is in grave need of training. Your training . . ."

"My training . . ."

"Get the pharmacopoeia. And would you happen to have a quarter grain taste anywhere around this place?"

"My training . . ." Doctor Grabow, rather more rumpled

than usual, wandered off a step or two; then turned. "Beg pardon? A taste . . . ?"

"Go on, you fat fool." Blight waved an impatient hand. "Just fetch me your black bag. I'll look for myself."

"My training . . ." the Doctor rode off on his favorite fantasy, mindlessly wandering off to do Blight's bidding.

The little man, bald as an egg, sat in his room at the Y, writing a very, very important letter on his own personal, beige-tinted stationery. Such love and tender care he lavished upon each word, and O so neat: a single mis-stroke of his pen and he must start all over again.

He'd written letters such as this one before, but this was one of the few times that he'd had an address to mail the letter to. That's what made this one so 'specially important. So exciting to write:

Oh, My Fierce Mistress,

he paused to savor the salutation; then plunged on.

I have obeyed your orders and here I am in SF, just like you told me to come here so that I could plead for an in-person interview with you. Which is what I want more than anything else.

After all these weeks of wonderful corresponding with you, I hope you don't mind my saying that I feel like I know you already. I am ready to be your slave. Let me kiss your feet also anything else you should command. And if I do not please you exactly how you want to be pleased, then give me the whip and make me suffer. You know which whip I mean. I mean the whip with the three-tongued lash, each lash with a little horsehair knot at the end. The whip you wrote me about in your last four letters. They were wonderful letters. So are you wonderful.

And that is why I have come to SF. And I only hope and pray that you will let me come to see you in-person. As you know, I have only this P.O. Box Number to write you at, so please write to me right away care of the Y, Room 101, and tell me where you are.

Also I did just what you said and took all my money out of the bank and brought it with me. All my savings I will gladly spend on you. And you can make me your devoted, cringing, crawling, dog-slave, personal maid to do with howsoever you please. Please.

You told me that I should tell you my most embarrassing secret, so just to show you what a good, obedient, well-schooled slave I am, I will tell you. And I only hope that you won't be too disgusted or anything like that. But you told me to tell you, so here goes.

I only hope and pray that you will like it and let me come and see you. Here goes.

Since I first answered your advertisement in the newspaper and since then I have written you ten letters and you have written me five letters back. Well these five letters you wrote me are my most precious possession. And when I feel so bad that I wish to end this dreadful, long, unhappy farce, my life, then I take off all my clothes and I take one of your letters, each time I use a different one, and I rub it all over me, your letter. Call me crazy but I don't care. Because I can feel your strong hand on my naked skin. I feel your hand right through your handwriting. I feel it so strong it makes me shiver and when I close my eyes I can almost see that hand of yours, no doubt in soft black glacé gloves. And I see that hand raised over my defenseless, exposed, entirely at your mercy Private Parts. And I can't tell you how much better I feel after I think about that for a while. I mean the punishment. . . .

The little man continued on in this vein for several beige pages, concluding with a

prayerful request for a meeting at your very earliest convenience. Could that be tomorrow night? I beg you, Mistress. Tomorrow night, at eight o'clock in the restaurant across the street from this Y. The place is called Mama

Lion's Steaks, Chops, and Fried Chicken. I will be there at one of the back tables. You can recognize me by the boutonniere I will wear.

Please please please come.

I am your wholly devoted slipper-sucker,

Mimi

ps—I love you.

Blight threw back his head and laughed. But Katy was kinder. She read Mimi's letter twice.

"I never thought the little homosqueak would actually have the nerve to come."

"I'd imagine that it gets very lonely in Nome," Spenser wiped the tears from his eyes. "Every Mimi needs to get away every now and then, I dare say."

"But has he any money?" Katy pretended she cared. "Should I dress?"

"Indeed you should." Spenser put a match to Mimi's letter, and the evidence went up in smoke; while Mimi appeared at Mama Lion's, promptly at five-thirty and made for a table in the dim back of the convenient Restaurant and Cocktail Lounge, Mixed Drinks A Specialty.

But not the only specialty. . . .

. . . Katy lifted her skirt. "Now Spenser, will you just look at that. I'm still black and blue from that Goddamned sadist. *Look Spenser . . . !*"

"Yes dear, I am looking," said Spenser obligingly. Unfortunately he needed most of his attention to fix the studs in his boiled dinner shirt. But he was doing his Dagwood best. "My, my dear. Isn't that something? Who would have believed that the old ape could still wallop so hard?"

"Someone is going to pay for this," Katy said ominously,

ignoring the fact that Grabow, M.D., had already paid liberally and in advance. "Someone is going to feel my heel . . . tonight the shoe is on the other foot, right Spenser?"

"Right-O, dear. Now you'd best hurry up. It's after eight."

"He'll wait," said she, rummaging through her wardrobe. "He'll wait for me, forever."

That Katy. For all her disorganized, feminine ways, she was a thoroughly satisfactory partner in crime. Since the collapse of their fortune, she had shown all sorts of initiative. She was against all the laws. She violated and got violated without a qualm, and contrary to all the sociological statistics, depravity did not make her less loving nor less fit for married life. If anything, the intimacy of illegality married them better, deeper, more lastingly than any engraved matrimonial convention.

Blight patted Katy's lacerated rump. Birds of a concupiscent feather. Katy, especially. She was always burning, always on the edge of orgasm. A lewd wink was quite enough to make her come.

Wonderful, passionate, solemn Katy. Possessed, well-bred, well-schooled Katy. A Rare, an Excellent, a Great Queen among women. And yet, despite her lofty station, Katy, not less than any demented slut, remained King Kong's concubine: a she-ass ready to be driven mad by any erection, real or fancied.

To be sure, she was a carnivorous she-ass. Even as a mediocrity, she couldn't help being exceptional. Of this, Spenser was very well aware. Although circumstances and the monomania of Public Demand usually forced her into the Submissive Role, she could crack a ten-foot bullwhip with no little expertise. There had been more than one occasion, Spenser could recall, when some bully who had bought her to beat her, didn't, but instead betrayed himself by a slip of his lamb's heart. Then Katy was not slow to seize the advantage. She changed places like another woman would change her dress. And then with the bully's own rod, Katy could coo quite another tune. And you may be sure that she knew all the words.

One might be excused from the impertinence of wondering how it was that Blight continued his nearly absolute dominance over such a formidable woman.

Blight's advantage was ridiculously simple. It may be given in a single sentence.

Hardly ever did he expire in her presence.

On her birthday, Madame Dubois, of the Comédie-Française, noted in her private diary on September 12th, 1775, the day she was fifty-six (56) years old:

> I have just calculated the grand total of 16,527 sexual partners. For an entire week, I have been assiduously searching my memory and my old diaries (I have fortunately been allowed to preserve the complete set) and this figure is as nearly complete as I can estimate.

Now remember, Katy was only twenty-two and a half years old, and but at the start of her professional career, as it were. No claim is made that she was a serious rival to the illustrious Madame Dubois. Nevertheless, we may note that during the first three months, or *trimester period*—as it is henceforth designated—of their enterprising attempt to recoup their financial fortunes, Katy had intercourse (carnal) with what was calculated at a mean of 1.03 persons (individual contacts) per diem; within the trimester period, to be fixed at 30, 31, and 26 diems. Respectfully.

Or to put it less precisely, the large bed in the furnished apartment that she shared with Spenser was beginning to take

on some of the qualities of a National Park. She was beginning, for example, to attract her *habitués*, her Repeaters, her
Special Friends who returned again and again to wander up
her garden path.

She was a seminal trough. Spenser didn't judge her
harshly. In truth, her excesses were his particular pride, not to
mention his only source of income.

"Katy, it's ten minutes to nine!"

"I'm coming, Spenser. Just let me strap this thing on,
and I'm ready."

Mimi tapped his
jumpy left eye with a lacquered forefinger. "Behold," he an-
nounced in a pretentious hush. "Behold, a nervous tic where
once a flower bloomed."

Tipsy Mimi in a spanking new blue suit, blue tie, white
shirt, and ill-fitting toupee. Three hours of mixed drinks, while
waiting for the Mistress Käi to arrive . . . plus the heady rapture that comes to the spectator when he rises from his seat
and climbs across the footlights to appear on the stageset of his
own imagination. Playing such an important part in his own
fantasy had made him giddy, unusually bold, and hyper-
enthusiastic. He burbled blissfully on, describing his desires
and deceptions in all the detail that even Spenser could ask for.

The appetizer was served, followed by the soup, which in
turn was replaced by the main course . . . but Mimi feasted
on the tigerish twinkle in the blue-violet eyes of the tall,
haughty, tyrannical woman seated across from him. He licked
up all the contempt at the table. He gnawed gratefully at the
few smiles, cold bones, that Katy tossed his way. He recited
his submission, breathlessly, uninterrupted by a single forkful
of food. The waiter simply put a dish down in front of him,
and ten to fifteen minutes later removed the dish and returned

it to the kitchen for reheating and eventual resale to someone else.

Mimi never minded. He was perfectly satisfied with the opportunity to converse, if not *with*, then at least *under*, the dangerous eyes of his furious Mistress, his Royal Employeress . . . Kween Käi of the aggressive, manhunting, dirty-book tribe of Tame-a-zons.

Käi sat calmly across the table, chewing her meat with big, strong, white teeth. (Recall that once Katy had been a rich girl, and no rich girl *ever* has bad teeth.) Sharp, gleaming teeth, visible inside the carmine hell of her lips; those teeth did their job, efficiently masticating with awful deliberateness; the jaw muscles rippled, her throat worked with a regular ingestive-flex. And all the while, her pitiless gaze examined the silly, simpering, girlishly grotesque Mimi, who simply couldn't stop babbling.

". . . and I've been an undertaker for almost sixteen years! It's just so fantastic that I can hardly believe it myself. Of course it isn't that I particularly like the profession, but when you're trained for nothing else . . . I mean, what else could I do to earn a living? So . . ."

"Have you ever considered entering domestic service?" asked Katy, rather quietly. This, one of the very few things she said all evening.

Mimi's jaw hung open. He was absolutely amazed. She seemed to understand him so well.

"Well . . . 'pon my soul! I mean, it's really funny that you should pick out *that particular occupation*, because it happens that I do have this kind of daydream. I mean, I guess that's what you'd call it." Mimi cocked his perky little head. His thin, bloodless lips turned a trifle smug. "You know, sometimes I think about other things besides coffins."

"Yes?" Spenser's voice had the slightest Teutonic edge to

it. Most effective for the impersonal-personal question. "What other sort of things besides coffins?"

"Well . . . you're going to think that I'm crazy, but . . ." he sneaked a shy peek at Katy, who went on chewing, swallowing, cutting another piece of meat, putting it in her mouth, and so on. A most disinterested Mistress. Mimi decided to take a chance. "Of course I know that it's going to be awfully difficult at my age, and all that, but really, I've been thinking that maybe I would look around and see if I can't find something in that line. I mean, I know that I'm completely inexperienced and everything, but you couldn't find a more willing worker, and . . ."

Katy continued gobbling. Mimi had been through this monologue at least three times since they'd joined him at this table in the back. Obviously, he loved to fill out Application Forms. . . .

". . . comb her long hair, and if I snagged it even ever-so-slightly—of course you know that I would be as careful as I could—but say just for the sake of discussion, say that I accidentally snagged my Mistress' hair, while attending to her toilet. Well, I think that no punishment that she might mete out to me would be too severe. I wouldn't care so long as it amused her a little, because what is a lady's personal maid for if not to amuse her lady? After all, any personal maid could snag her Mistress' hair, or fail to polish a boot to perfection . . . and no one is more of a Perfectionist than I am . . . but accidents will happen, and they do happen, and a personal maid can only show how sorry she is by suffering for her lady's entertainment . . . Oh Madame!" Mimi broke off, addressing the austere Mistress directly, instead of obliquely through her dangerous Factotum, the steely, heavily scarred Baron. "Madame, please. I beg you to give me just a hint. Would it please you . . . would you like it if I were punished?"

"... most stringently,"
Katy had memorized his speech. Now she recited it along with
him. Her expression cool as jade.

"Punished and made to understand that I tolerate no
disobedience. *Nein ich misbehäben, elsen kums a torterun-
schrass!*" She lifted a cruel eyebrow. "You understand me, I
think, eh?"

Mimi nodded dumbly. He didn't trust his voice. He
breathed deeply, and thought very fleetingly of concentration
camps. Without realizing it, he must have been trying to crawl
under the table, for Spenser's iron grip brought him up short.

"The Madame countenances no public display."

"Please . . . my arm!" Mimi grimaced apologetically
through his tears. Blight released his arm, and Mimi, confused
and flustered, took a quarter-turn in Katy's direction and made
a stiff little half-bow. He was easily influenced by a Prussian
accent. Unfortunately, his bow was a little too abrupt, and his
toupee slipped over his left eye. Rakish pup . . . !

"Madame *must* forgive me, or I will not go on living."
He dabbed at his papery forehead; his bluish lips puckered. He
was salivating effusively. . . .

". . . will forgive me? You will let me come and . . ."
Käi crooked
a bloodred talon. A string ran from the first knuckle of that
dreadful finger to the dorsal aperture between the fifth and
sixth buttons of Mimi's shirt. And then, without the slightest
variance of expression, without a wink or a leer or even a
ghost of a smile, she crooked the finger, pulled the string,
popped Mimi's cork, and his heart came rushing out after.

"Stuff it back in your pants, you pig!" Käi hissed. Then
she stood up, towering over him. He worshiped with wet,
spaniel eyes. His muzzle was wet, his paws were trembling;
his breath, irregular. Heartbeat, rapid.

"Good dog!" she smiled at him for the first time, and

Mimi might have rolled over and bepissed himself in doggy-joy, had he not feared the Mistress' disapproval. He understood perfectly well what was meant by Public Displays. He knew how and why to be circumspect. But could you blame him for wanting to tell her. How much he needed. Also other things about himself. Could you blame him for wanting to tell her? So that she would realize that he was her devoted, little, helpless, wretched, grateful Mimi. Her menial. Her. . . .

Her fragrance made him swoon, nearly. She stood right beside his chair. His eyes, when he dared turn his head, were level with her hard crotch. Her words, the divine growl, came down to him from Heaven. Naturally, he bowed his head.

"I am withdrawing now," she said. "I'm going to straighten my stockings and feed my nightingales. I've a furry nest of them between my legs, you know. Never mind how much you'd give to see it. I'm not interested. My manager, the Baron, handles my affairs. When I return, in just a few minutes, according to the Baron's advice, I shall reject you (Mimi shriveled), or I will accept you. And if I do take you into my Service, be forewarned . . . I intend to mistreat you. Yes, dear, yes . . ." Käi spoke so softly that Spenser, only a few feet away, had some difficulty in overhearing. She spoke directly into Mimi's tender, rosebud earlet. Her words making spicy little puffs in the air.

". . . yes, dear," she was saying. "Yes, you'll see." She was bending over him, her arm casually yoking his thin shoulder. "Yes, you'll see how I transform you from a mortician into a proper maid. Don't you doubt it. I will m*i*s*t*r*e*a*t* you. Only wait and see . . ." The inflection she gave the verb, *mistreat*, was a delicious act of cruelty in itself.

Then, with a swish of her black satin skirt, and the painfully sharp rat-a-tat-tat of her pencil-thin, seven-inch-high heels, she was gone, leaving Mimi to gag on his vice.

"FIVE HUNDRED!" the Baron kicked his shin, and Mimi snapped out of his revery with a high-pitched yelp. "Five hundred dollars, and don't be all night making up your mind. Everything must be settled before the Tigeretta returns from the Powder Room. Hurry!"

Mimi gulped a glass of iced water. The serpentine dueling scar that decorated the Baron's brutal, meaty face, distracted Mimi from giving the financial problem the undivided attention it deserved. It was, as previously noted, his life savings: a sum about as pitiful as the man who'd spent his life saving it . . . *that scar was the most fascinating disfigurement* . . . Mimi wondered if he dared ask whether the Baron's opponent had suffered as much. Probably a good deal more, judging from the Baron's menacing air. Mimi turned all goosey. A sudden chill made him tremble.

But brought him no respite.

"Did you hear me? I said, *Five Hundred Dollars!*"

"But sir, I don't have that much . . ."

"You liar . . . !"

"No! I swear it to you. I don't have . . ."

"Well damn you, how much do you have? How much?" The Baron was so urgent, so pressing. So . . . Hurry! Fast! Quick, how much? You'd better skip . . . the train is getting ready to leave. "How much?"

Mimi said a number. The Baron apparently didn't believe his ears. "How much did you say?" A train whistle blew behind his yellow eyes.

Mimi gave up bargaining. He said another number, twice as much as the first number. Head bowed, he waited for the Baron to accept or spurn his offering. The Baron's saffron eyes regarded him levelly.

"It's all the money I have. I swear it on my mother's head, may she be remanded to Hell if I'm lying."

"You gave me to understand that you had drawn out your entire capital," the Baron bit off the end of a cigar, rolled the savory tube around in his mouth, and never took his eyes off the sweat-soaked little man, the little Supplicant across the table. "Your life savings . . . ?"

The train began to move out of the station, but Mimi wasn't on it.

"Baron, please accept me. Four hundred and fifty dollars is all I have . . . I worked so hard . . . most of my life . . . but I haven't been able to save . . . four hundred and fifty . . . ? Please?"

"How did you expect to return to Nome?"

A long silence. Finally Mimi peeped. "I have an airplane ticket."

"Hand it over." Blight took the ticket, slipped it into his wallet. "Face value of the airline ticket is forty-one dollars, fifty cents . . ."

"But without my ticket, how will I get back home?"

"You'll have to drop me a postcard and let me know how. I'm curious about that, myself. However, more to the immediate point, you are eight dollars and fifty cents too poor to afford the Madame."

Mimi whined. "But only eight dollars and fifty cents . . . couldn't you make an exception? I mean . . . *I haven't got eight dollars and fifty cents!*" he suddenly cried out in real anguish. He chased frantically down the platform after the departing train. Then, do or die, ride or bleed to death on the cinder-bed between the tracks. Mimi shut his eyes and leaped. . . .

". . . Four hundred and fifty dollars, cash, plus a negotiable airline ticket, face value, forty-one dollars and fifty cents." The Baron added up Mimi's life, while

Mimi, across the table, hung in the balance. Eight dollars and fifty cents.

Mimi didn't open his eyes. He felt himself falling. But Blight caught him just in time. With deft fingers, he slipped the wristwatch off Mimi's limp wrist. The watchband looked to be platinum. Of course it was just a guess. Blight didn't have a jeweler's glass at hand. But he was willing to take the chance.

"Welcome aboard," the Baron screwed his monocle into his left eye. Always a Prussian stickler for formality. "May I congratulate you, little lady. You have been accepted as Mistress Käi's very own body servant."

Mimi smiled gratefully through a mist of tears. There was a great lump in his throat.

"Will I be permitted to wear my own uniform, or does the Mistress have her own personal livery? I mean, so many grand ladies do . . ."

"Yes. Well that's something that you can take up with your Madame. Who knows how she might want you attired?"

"My goodness, yes! You're right. Why, I never even thought of that . . . ! But in any case we must stop for just a sec at the Y across the street. I've left my wig in my room, and I'm dying to try it on in front of . . . I mean, this will be the first time I've ever worn a wig," bashful Mimi scuffled his feet under the table. "This will be the first time, *in mixed company.*"

"We'll get your wig." Spenser signaled for the check. He noticed Katy coming out of the Powder Room, across the restaurant. She walked toward them slowly, stiff-legged.

"... and I have a little cap that goes with it. You know the kind, all frilly and . . ."

"What color?" Blight wondered politely, eying Käi over Mimi's shoulder.

"Why it's white, of course. Wait till you see it. It's all Frenchy and it ties under the chin. Even if the Madame has a uniform for me, I'm sure she'll let me wear the little cap too, because you know it doesn't only make me look just exactly like a French maid, but it also holds my wig on. No matter what terrible ordeal the Madame puts me through, I won't have to worry about my wig falling off. Not so long as I have my cap tied on."

Spenser's cigar—still unlit—made a soft, wet *plop* as he pulled it out of his mouth. "Of course you may wear the wig and the French maid's cap," he condescended so languidly, and Katy who had come up behind Mimi's chair, finished what he had started to say.

"Of course you may wear the French cap. It will go very well with the satin and scarlet lace apron . . ."

"I will have hose?"
Mimi didn't dare to turn around for fear the spell might break.

"You shall have hose. Black mesh. Silk stockings held up by not less than six suspenders. Six on each leg, that is. O we shall play, little vixen . . . ah what games I have planned for you!" Käi's breasts brushed the back of Mimi's bald head. His toupee lay, unnoticed, in his lap.

"Little Vixen, little Minx!" the Baron mocked softly. The light glanced off his glass eye, blinding Mimi, who sat very still, not minding at all. Something like a queer, twisted little smile played around the corners of his mouth; his narrow, middle-aged face.

The Baron casually stretched out his right hand—he might have been reaching for another cigar—and carefully grasped Mimi's tiny, nut-hard nipple, his fingernails biting through Mimi's wash 'n' wear white shirt. He pinched. Mimi squealed mildly.

"Oh Baron . . . !"
"Yes," Spenser promised him. "Yes, my dear, you shall

have an ample bosom before we're done with you. Two snowy white breasts, a full handful each. Two brown, soft-nosed titties to make you tingle . . ." He rolled Mimi's taut little nipple twixt thumb and index fingers, his voice was gentle and caressing. Mimi closed his eyes again, and sighed.

The Baron's fingernails nipped with sudden cruelty, pinching the tender flesh. . . .

Mimi's eyes stayed closed. He seemed to feel nothing. The queer smile played on and off his face.

"We'll make a proper lady out of you yet, Sweetheart." Käi rapped her knuckles playfully on his pate, and the Baron tweaked his teat one last time. "I know ways to make them grow," he teased, and blew a stream of cigar smoke into Mimi's blissful face.

The little man was still coughing when the waiter brought their check. Blight paid with Mimi's money. Then he took one of Mimi's arms. Käi took the other.

"Let's hurry right home," she urged, and Spenser nodded. Mimi in the middle. He moved like a clockwork doll, but Blight and Katy held on to him. Just in case something went wrong with his cuckoo-cuckoo.

VII

Magick me do! the proud young witch went down on her knees to pray. O please don't use it all! O let me have some, please. . . .

Certainly you may have some. But only wait a minute until I'm done . . . let me finish doing myself . . . there. Done. Alright. Sit down. Now. I'll do you magick. . . . Say how much you want?

All I can get, the Witch told him. The rosy flesh on her bare arms glowed in the lamplight. Her veins crawled green. Do me a little more she pleaded with her dark eyes. Tonight I need all I can get . . . have you magick enough to make me fifteen years old again?

Fifteen, going on sixteen? he laughed. Yes, I'll give you a few grams extra . . . since you want it so badly. But first, there's something that I want from you.

What?

Don't tremble so. I only want a kiss.

Ah . . . gladly.

Well then, to it! Lift up my tail and kiss me!

". . . and you're absolutely certain that there won't be any complications? Now you're sure?" Doctor Grabow detained Blight in the vestibule, plucking at the Wizard's sleeve. "The child hasn't run away from home or anything? You understand, I can't afford any trouble. . . ."

Blight's laughter shattered two wineglasses on the top shelf of the kitchen cupboard. Doctor Grabow would find them in the morning. Tonight, his mind was on other shattered matters.

Blight peeled the old man's frightened fingers off his overcoat sleeve. "Grabow, I have told you several times, there is

137

nothing for you to be afraid of. Everything, everything, *everything* has been arranged. Now go on, you're wasting your own time. She belongs to you. But only for tonight. Go on, Grabow. I can assure you the morning will be upon you all too soon. Hurry. Tonight she is yours . . ."

". . . I am yours!" sobbed Mimi, the new French maid. He knelt in his underwear, at the booted feet of Käi, Kruel Mistress of Bonhaven. From her gloved hands he received the wig of flaming red hair. Mistress Käi, a bizarre and exotic beauty, her black satin dress was skintight; her knee-length boots had seven-inch heels, and shiny silver spurs—bright, sharp little rowels that jingled when she nudged Mimi with her foot.

"Turn around. I'll have a look at your rump, my girl." Käi fondled her riding crop. Poor Mimi, squeaking with terror, made haste to turn himself around. . . .

"WELCOME TO FET-TERLAND," the Baron's voice came over the loudspeaker mounted above the bed.

"Who told you to turn your head?" the Mistress flared. "I said I wanted a look at your backside, and you dare disobey me by showing your face?"

"EVERY HEAD-STRONG, SELF-WILLED, UNDISCIPLINED AND SAUCY RED-HEADED WENCH NEEDS TO BE TRAINED. TAUGHT HOW TO SERVE TEA. . . . SHE MUST BE BROUGHT TO HEEL . . ." the Baron's guttural accent rang through Käi's mysterious chamber with the toneless echo of a torture-chamber voice counting the strokes; a disembodied voice from the terrible dungeons, the subterranean corridors. . . .

". . . BOUND HAND AND FOOT. TIED, GAGGED, BOUND UPSIDE

DOWN, INSIDE OUT. SUBJUGATED, HUMILIATED,
STRIPPED OF . . ."

"All those clothes you're hiding in," Käi commanded.
"Ridiculous for a girl like you to wear men's underwear, men's
shoes. Quick now, peel! I've a more suitable costume for you
to put on."

"OBEY!" the Baron bel-
lowed over the public address system.

"OBEY!" the Baron
roared.

Mimi tore at his undershorts. "I will! I will!" he whimpered. "Don't whip me again, please. I will . . . do anything . . .
everything! I will . . . !"

Put your little foot,

your little foot,
Put your little foot right here,
And shuffle-step
Shuffle, shuffle. Step and shuffle . . .

". . . love your hair," murmured Doctor Grabow, inhaling
her dark fragrance. Then he drew the rubber hood over Cay's
head. "There, there my sweet, my pretty, my good little girl."
The old fumbler, Grabow, gasped and greedily sucked air. He
panted and heaved as though he had just run a mile . . . but if
he had, he hadn't been running after Cay. Neither did she
struggle against him, but, as she'd been taught at Miss Muffin's
Wednesday-afternoon dancing class, she sat like a proper
young lady, on the edge of the couch in the living room of the
apartment across the street from her highschool. And no one
could have guessed that her class had let out more than half a
decade ago.

"And you say that you're sixteen, dear?" Breathless

Grabow could not stop asking questions. "Only sixteen . . . ?"

"No sir, I'm fifteen and a half, and I . . ."

"There!" cried Grabow triumphantly, crowing loudly right in the middle of an asthma attack. And why shouldn't he? Asthma was no great novelty, but he'd never before had Cay. *In the bag!* His puffy fingers drew the hood completely over her head; nimble fingers, this was one of the few jobs his surgeon's fingers hadn't botched. In a twinkling he'd tied a granny knot into the drawstring that ran around her neck.

"Can you breathe, precious?"

Cay's voice, though audible, was heavily muffled. "Not very well, sir. . . ."

"You'll get used to the hood," Doctor Grabow leered, though no one could see him. "You'll get used to that choking feeling, yes you will, my naughty little bad birdie . . . my fine, spirited pony. My . . . Oh my!" He simply had to stop for a moment. His heart was going so fast that he feared it would break out of his breast. Not that he was much worried about Death. *But not tonight!* He most certainly did not want to die before morning.

"Alright now," he was back in action after only a few seconds' respite. "Alright, put your hands together . . ."

"Please don't hurt me . . . sir." She showed her perfectly natural girlish fear for the first time, and Grabow could have kissed her feet in gratitude.

"Why, I wouldn't hurt you . . . not *you,* my dear."

Obediently, the teenager held out her arms without further fuss. It was probably fortunate that the hood prevented her from seeing the beet-red face of the overpassionate Doctor as he buckled the restraining straps on her slim, delightfully girlish, pale, fluttering wrists.

"Now, my dear young lady," Grabow wheezed. "And now . . ."

Shuffle,
shuffle,
shuffle, step and
shuffle, glide, and shuffle.

". . . and now, take off those repulsive undershorts and let me see your frail, pale, hairy body, my young Miss!" snarled the Master-Mistress, Lordess, and Lady Whipsman, the stern and beauteous ruler of Manacle Manor. She cracked a nine-foot hippo whip with wonderful skill, not three inches from Mimi's ear.

"Hip-hop! Now take off those shoes and socks. Nasty. . . . There. Better. Now . . ." she pointed to a gauzy pile on the chair. "Into your working clothes, Mimi mine. I am in the mood to teach you your duties."

Mimi looked at the pile of lacy, silky underwear, then back to Käi. "You're going to make me wear *those?*" he asked helplessly.

Käi unlimbered her long whip. "Indeed I am," she told him without excessive rancor, with a smile, even. And then
CRACK!
the metal stud at the tip of the snaky black whip bit deep into Mimi's naked backside.

"Is it your intention to keep me waiting all night?" she raged at him while the tears ran down his cheeks. "I will not be served by an improperly dressed, potbellied, French maid! Neither will I be patient very much longer . . . !"

She held the thick, silk-wrapped stock of the whip in her hand, but the long leather tongue snaked over her legs and along the floor, rippling expectantly, and of its own volition. . . . How are such things possible?

Mimi didn't pause to puzzle it out. He began drawing on the unfamiliar, though oft-imagined, intimate articles of a lady's maid's attire. Fast as ever he could. Black scanties, and stage hosiery, rubber-foam bra cups, fancy garters that were too tight and had sharp metal clasps that chewed on the soft flesh of his hairy thighs.

"Come here, you silly bitch, and I'll show you how to lace yourself into this . . ." Käi held the vicious whip in one hand. In the other, she held the most exciting corset that Mimi had ever seen. French Broche, whalebone struts, hooks and eyelets threaded with long, purple, catgut laces.

"Come here, little one. . . ."

At last. Alone in the *chambre* with the Mistress. She, seated on her throne beside her dressing table, ordered Mimi closer. *Now she's going to eat me*, he thought obscurely. And respectfully lowering his eyes, he approached. . . .

The Baron's iron claw reached out from nowhere and took a firm handhold of the flabby flesh around Mimi's midriff.

"That's close enough."

"Have him turn around and put his hands over his head." The Mistress suddenly seemed so distant. In contrast, the Baron stood so close to Mimi that the poor, mistreated, terrified Maid could not help but see the thick features of the Baron's brutal, saber-slashed face begin to droop and melt under the hellish, stunning, bright and very hot lights.

A face melting. A prominent scar, drooping, spreading, dripping like wax . . . it was all just exactly the way that Mimi had imagined it would be.

"Turn!" the Baron commanded curtly. The man's proximity made Mimi to prickle all over. "Put your hands over your head and hold on to that bracket. Hold on . . . don't let go!"

"*Don't* . . . !" Käi repeated the Baron's warning. Mimi couldn't be sure, but he thought he felt the cold tip of the hippo whip tickling him down around his lower limbs.

"Take a deep breath . . ." the steel grip of the Baron drew the laces tighter, inexorably tighter. The corset gripped him like a vise. Squeezed tighter and ever tighter. The Baron continued to draw the catgut strings in tighter. . . .

"Oh not so tight!" gasped Mimi. "Please . . . can't breathe . . . Oh, plea . . ."

". . . sure varies with the individual," Auntie Grabow was saying pedantically. "One man's pleasure is some little girl's pain!" Auntie illustrated his lecture with pinches and slaps and unnecessary cruelties. After many a torment, he'd unbuckled and rebuckled a wide belt around Cay's waist; a cunning little brass ring hung from each side of the belt. The Discipline Hood still covered her head, and the restraining cuffs were strapped behind her. Blind and helpless, Cay stumbled after Auntie Grabow.

A brand new dog collar encircled her neck, and clipped to this collar was a thin leather leash. Auntie, ahead of her, tugged impatiently.

"Don't dawdle, dumpling," merry Auntie gave the leash a savage pull. The collar served as a choker: each jerk drew it a little tighter.

Sightless Cay. She tried to keep up, but every false step drew the collar tighter. She sputtered but could not cry out.

She heard many bells ringing, singing, falling away. . . . She heard Auntie cry out, "You're malingering, my child. I'll have to chastise you for that."

It seemed to hooded Cay that she was following Auntie Grabow through a black rubber maze, and the further along they went, the denser the uterine labyrinth became: the less air there was for Cay to breathe. And though she was trotting —a dangerous pace for a girl who can't see where she's going —still Auntie urged her on even faster.

"Come, come . . . you naughty girl! You mustn't keep my Horsey waiting. You'll be sorry if you do."

And strangled if she didn't. The dog collar prevented her

from swallowing. The bells, big bells and little cracked bells, louder and louder in her ears. Cay wondered if Auntie meant to kill her. Wondered about Auntie's Horsey. . . .

". . . tighter! Baron, make it tighter!"

"You're killing me!" screamed Mimi in a high, thin squeak.

"I say *tighter!* Ah, Baron . . . only you know how much I like my maids tightly laced."

"Yes, Mistress, it is my pleasure," rumbled the Baron. He gripped the catgut corset strings, and put his knee in the small of Mimi's back. "Hang on to that bracket, Mimi. I'm going to nip you in another inch or two."

"Nooooooo . . . Oh no! Oh I can't stand it . . . !"

"But you must stand it!" Auntie's stringent tone brooked no schoolgirl's nonsense. No whining. No begging. No mercy. . . . "And you'd best understand that, my wilful young lady. You will take your punishment exactly as I order you to. And you will thank me for it, before we're done this evening. Oh you'll thank me, I'll warrant you . . ."

Cay heard a wand whistling through the air, *thwicker!*

"Yiiiiii!" she shrieked as Auntie's birch flicked lightly against the back of her bare legs.

"It is well that you learn now, this, one of the unalterable facts of life." Auntie Headmistress stood right behind Cay, and with a pudgy index finger, traced the welt that was rising to commemorate the last lash . . . or better put, the most recent stroke, for the *last* cut was still far in the future. It could not be much after midnight, Cay calculated. And she belonged to Grabow till dawn. Till *forever* is finally over. . . .

"Learn it and never forget it," Auntie was saying, and he

did an unexpected thing with the hand that had been playing up and down the back of Cay's leg. An unexpected and frightful thing.

Cay screamed as good as any Auntie could ask, and got rewarded with a giggle instead of a swat.

"As I was saying . . . Figure Training is an arduous, painful, fatiguing, humiliating course of study. But it brings its own rewards."

thwicker-thwick!

"You didn't hear that one coming, did you?" Auntie chuckled dryly. "Posture erect, if you please, smart young Missy. Erect, I say!" Such an inflexible Auntie. "And it is not permitted to sigh in my presence unless I so order you. But I *didn't* order you to, did I? Answer!"

"No, Auntie . . ."

"Posture erect! Two wrongs do not make a single right! Oh I must educate you. We'll begin by taking the hood off. Your saucy backside has earned you *cinquenta* lashes. And before I give them to you, I want you to look at what you're going to get . . . what I have waiting for you. Oh, my pretty pussy, I'll be so happy to see you cry."

"Well, I'm not crying yet," said Cay rebelliously. That was her temper again. The words were no sooner out than she regretted them.

"But not half so much as you are going to regret them," Auntie embraced her from behind, hugged her with surprising tenderness. "Oh, sweetheart, you're not crying yet . . . but you will be soon!"

With his fat, venal fingers, puffy and dead white, Grabow unbuckled the dog collar, tossed it away; then tugged at the bow under her chin. The rubber hood peeled back, exposing her hot, moist features. Her raven hair had curled into shiny black ringlets pasted against her smooth forehead.

Cay blinked. The electric light was so bright after the

hood. Her large eyes filled with tears, and it was a long moment before the objects around her swam back into focus. Curious . . . but the first thing she saw, when her sight returned, was not the monstrous Auntie Grabow, it was Grabow's Horsey.

Cay stared. She knew immediately, without asking any questions, she knew what that thing was. Because it was so hideous, so bloodstained, foul and all spattered with horror . . . ?

Not at all. It was just an ordinary sawhorse; one of the plain, pinewood variety favored by carpenters, house painters, everyday folk. Of course not every sawhorse is fitted out with four loops of tarred rope—though that certainly is an efficient arrangement. Hands go through these two loops, feet through these two. A few yards of secondhand satin wrapped around the 2 x 4 cross-support. A nicety to prevent the sharp edges from cutting too deeply into the soft, the tender, the flesh that has not yet reached the age of legal consent.

"Up you go, little Cay. Up on Horsey . . ." Auntie tapped Cay's pert rump with the end of the birch. "Up, I say!"

Cay scrambled. Auntie, birch tucked under her arm, fixed the ropes around Cay's wrists and ankles. A most uncomfortable mount.

Cay spraddled on Horsey; her short skirt hiked up over her chubby, young backside. Black sheer panties stretched tightly across the uplifted, expectant buttocks.

SWACK!

Cay howled.

Auntie had switched switches; exchanged the green, budding birch for a whippy-ash plant.

SWACK! the second stroke ripped the black silken scanties. Cay screamed, and the cork-lined walls drank in her painful rhapsody.

"That's two," purred Auntie, giving Cay plenty of time to feel each stroke. "Only forty-eight more till graduation . . ."

"O no more, please no more. Give me no more." Cay wept.

"Persevere, child, persevere. We've lots more hours till morning. And I've all sorts of fun to teach you . . ."

". . . I'll teach you!" The pizzle-tipped hippo whip, the vicious black tongue, snapped; licked a lippet of flesh from Mimi's naked shoulder. The little lace cap had come off. The wig had slipped around so that the long red hair hung over Mimi's pinched, white face.

"Stand aside, Baron." The Mistress stood a few feet behind the sobbing new maid Mimi. He still clutched the overhead bracket. The Baron, bursting in his shirtsleeves, a most efficient assistant to the Mistress, moved away from the new girl.

"The slut needs a lesson!"

"*Ja!* Give it to him good!"

And the big whip cracked again.

Mimi sang out, and Käi growled with delight. "O, I enjoy this fellow. How long did you say I might keep him?"

"You may have him until dawn, Mistress." The Baron clicked his heels smartly. "Do with him as you please till then."

"No . . . no . . . no," mewed poor Mimi, not daring to move, but protesting feebly for the record. "I've changed my mind . . . please let me go."

"Not until morning."

CRACK! Käi made Mimi's bell to ring again. She never missed.

"Baron, will you be so kind as to proceed wtih the lacing." She turned and strolled back to her throne, reseated herself voluptuously, and recrossed her legs. "Proceed, Baron, proceed . . ."

The steel-boned corset, an impeccable vise in the Baron's strong hands, squeezed still another half-inch from the henna-tressed mortician.

This Mimi, hanging by his own hands; his thin arms were stiff and riddled with sharp pins and needles of pain. A trickle of blood shyly crawled down from his welted shoulder to the padded cup of his bra. His mouth tasted badly of copper and burnt leaves. His eyes were dazzled with delicious bursts of Roman candles, exploding in slow motion. The queerest thoughts fell through his suddenly unlimited mind. And a voice rolled around inside his head, saying over and over, *Natural lamb*

rolled wet skin natural lamb. Rolled skin.
Natural lamb.

It was the voice of Mistress Mystery, his brutiful tyrant, coming to him from a great distance, at great expense, in empirical echoes, booming hollowly . . . "Very good Baron. That's tight enough for the time being . . . and now, Mimi, you may lower your arms. Frumpet! Did you hear me? I said you may lower your arms!"

"Thank you, Mist . . . " Mimi released the bracket and crumpled to the floor in a dead faint. It was only to be expected. Nothing in his meager past had prepared him for such ecstasies: too many years had he starved on the thin gruel of his own, unvitalized phantasies. His constitution simply couldn't stand the rich infusion of Käi's cruelties, and Bar Habvor's insatiable appetite. The loathsome dwarf, oily and ugly, lay like a lump in Käi's shimmering lap, hissing excitedly.

"O do this! Do that! Pull his up and down and do him, do!" The gibbering imp, all depraved inspiration: he spoke Käi's language.

"Yes," she translated for the Baron. "You will tie the little chit to the floor-pegs."

Blight looked at her curiously. He started to say something, but she urged him on to the task. "Oh do it, please . . . please, before he wakes up. I want to see the expression on his face when he comes to, spread-eagled on my floor. And we'll gag him, too . . ."

If the Baron had any reservations, he kept them to himself. He dragged Mimi over to the pegs, took four short lengths of rope out of his back pocket and bent to his work.

"And I'll get the gag . . ." Käi rose to help get Mimi ready. "I just want to see that look on his face when he opens his eyes and finds out that he can't move an inch, or make a peep."

The Baron whistled softly, ". . . sweetheart, I had no idea. Why, you're every bit as bad as I've always said you were. *Insatiable.*"

Katy had the agility to blush. "O well, it's just this once, Spenser. Usually it's the other way around . . ."

                                                    "this way!
And that way! Go this way! And that way,
                                        Go the other way
around!"

Auntie Grabow was insatiable. His eyes were glazed, and he was snorting.

"Mayn't I rest just a second? Please sir . . . only a second."

"We aren't tired already, are we? Not all tuckered out so soon?"

Cay staggered. She would have fallen if the ticklebar had not held her upright.

"Now then, my tearful young wretch," the wicked old Auntie mocked in his high, scratchy voice. "I'll stiffen your backbone for you! What you want is a touch of this . . . !"
                            "OH!"
"And this . . . !"
                            "OH OH OH!"
"And just a bit more of this . . . !"
                            Cay swooned. Unconscious,
she dangled at the end of her chain. Auntie observed her for a

moment with something like satisfaction. Then, a sudden and very disturbing thought occurred to him. Hurriedly, Doctor Grabow stepped up to her, and took her pulse.

Reassured by the heady beat—rapid but strong—Auntie set about rearranging Cay's limp body into position for the next exercise. Which would commence the instant the rosy-fleshed, dark-tressed, tempting, and helpless youngster opened her big, innocent eyes.

Grabow sank into his baronial chair, across the room, and waited for Cay to recover. Fifteen and a half years old, going on sixteen . . . Grabow took his own pulse.

VIII

It was, of course, a trick. Complicated, ingenious, extraordinarily effective. How it was managed, by mirrors, by hypnosis, by suggestive charms, or by perversions of natural laws, the thing to remember is, a good illusionist can make it happen every time. All he needs to know is the obvious. Once he recognizes your secret, he can magick you. And you should know that these men, these illusionmen, these Blights, have devised a System of Nomenclature and Classification whereby they can identify almost every dirty on first sight; print the image onto a thin, gelatin-treated, ultra-sensitized sheet of plastique; expose the sheet, or *transparency*, as it is sometimes called; and there you are . . . face to face, with a clear, durable, in-focus Lantern Slide. Magick? Yes.

But a trick, as well. A *prearrangement*, if you prefer. The noteworthy fact—considerations of wrong and white aside, for we are not morality specialists—brought out by this magickness that Blight was doing, and Katy was being . . . the magick was the magick of all great illusionists, which is not mumbo-jumbo magick, flash paper magick, sleight-of-hand, gypsy switch, or mystery man. . . .

It is only Blight, a self-convicted great illusionist of the first water. He needed only a wall or a screen to throw his shadow on . . . *his shadow,* impersonating *your vices.* His manipulations and your make-believes appear LARGER THAN LIFE, hand-illuminated, and posed in easily recognizable postures, positions, etc., etc.

Still, it was a trick. Just like dreams are tricks. And like movies, which are tricks based on tricks.

As Blight explained in his autobiographical *A Magickical Historee of Cinemalogy:*

151

"Given a wall to write on, all manner of monsters are possible."

Understand this, and it is possible to understand how magick, through some extravagant oversight, is blood relation to photography, the ubiquitous hobby of everyman . . . who knows not what he does.

They do not realize what magick they are fruttering about with; how they are making ghosts in the darkrooms . . . what does your average everyman know about that? And once in a while, by unfortunate accident, some lens-enthusiast adds a drop too much fixer solution, at a certain temperature, under certain variable conditions, under a certain sort of underground, in-closet curse; or maybe he just happens to look into the developing pan at the wrongest time, and there he sees a phantom or some other magick that he has inadvertently been tampering with—magick-doing, without knowing what he was doing—and then there is an explosion or a fire, sometimes a cherry bomb rigged up to the flash-gun on his camera, and the next time he snaps an indoor picture, he blows up. And one can only observe that accidents propagate themselves. Further, some people should leave magick entirely alone. Especially when they don't know what it is.

But if, like Blight for example, they do have cognizance of what they are about, there is a limitless fortune in magick, in trick photography. . . .

" . . . you think I'd sell you a pig in a poke?" Blight had poked more than one pork roll & sausage fancier into paying twice the price, and paying it in advance, using nothing but a pocket-sized Polaroid photograph of Katy. A photograph to be extracted from his wallet, at the crucial moment, with all possible ritual, and then placed face down, between Blight and whosoever haggled over how much Katy would cost.

"How much?"

"Turn the picture over and then we'll discuss arrangements."

Face down, all trump cards look alike.

"Go on, turn it over. Let's see if that's what you had in mind..."

TURN IT OVER

A competently composed photograph has validity turned any which way. It should be effective even when turned inside-out. Even when standing on her head.

"Is that her?" The bargain-hunters could be trusted to react according to type. Some wrung their hands, surreptitiously. Others tapped their swagger sticks against their boots, reflectively. Some scratched, some sweated, some salivated, some snickered and made lewd remarks. (Which Spenser always tried to remember: Katy loved him to repeat their comments, afterwards, verbatim.)

A photograph, fortunately for Blight's patience, is not so literal. Everyone is invited to see what they want to see, and Blight is not obliged to sell or pander anything to anyone. He need only sit back, and allow each man to take care of himself.

"Turn it over,"

was Blight's big trick.

You may examine this photograph. It is a genuine trick. You may pick it up and examine

it from all sides. Your curiosity solicited. See
if you can guess how the trick is done.

How to catch the double-image, and picture our Katy with all her hybrid appeal. How to trick the Boys into seeing *it*. What they wanted to see. It was easy.

"You know . . . " the clientele all brought their own contracts. "You know something . . . this girl is the spitting sister, almost, of the kind of girl I had in mind. This is fantastic . . . !"

And it certainly was. Fantastic. A single photograph of one girl. Very possibly Katy . . . but it was impossible to be sure. She was twisted into such a curious pose, an awkward but effective position, seminude (some described her as semicostumed: only one of the many, many points of view), and perched suggestively on what was, apparently, the shaggy back of some great, coarse animal.

And it certainly was fantastic. Every hot paw that handled the photograph saw the girl of his dreams.

FOR SALE

" . . . for the evening, if you think she might be what you're looking for."

"Might be, might be . . . " the Major hummed, studying the photo in his own peculiar fashion. He was an immaculate, wavy-faced, middle-aged psychopath, always dressed up tight in spiffy little business uniforms. Ties of regimental stripes, knotted correctly around his miserly stiff neck. His shirt was always clean, his pants had a permanent press, his expression was starched daily, his shoes were shined glossy every morning. He had mean and pointy little feet.

And best of all, he had a holohedral diamond, large as a walnut, attached to his watch-chain. No one knew where the Major's money came from, but anyone who cared enough to ask him, was welcome to know where he spent it.

"She just might be *the* girl, Blight. There's something

about her . . . " Something that keeps the Major's china-blue eyes stitched to the photograph, held carefully in his well-scrubbed hand; while around him, pretty girls in frilly, thigh-high skirts, dashed about in the electric darkness, carrying trays of drinks from the bar to the tiny tables around the nightclub.

A singer, a professionally smoky figure, in the center of the nightclub, sat in a pale yellow spotlight, strumming a guitar, accompanying Spenser, who sang his song right into the Major's eager ear.

> "Oh there was a gay trickster
> from Cooze,
> Sawed a lady in two, at the mews.
> When he grabbed for a section,
> It gave him an erection.
> But . . . *which half did he choose?*"

(Shuffle-step, Shuffle-shuffle.)

"Handsome haunches on this filly," the Major, still hooked to the photograph, answered Blight's question without having heard it. "Attractive blood-lines and all that . . . but see here, Blight, you're asking too much money, you know." The Major tried to chisel. All his life he had paid too much for everything, and tonight would not be an exception. Although, for a few minutes, the Major had the temerity to try. . . .

"I hope you're a reasonable man, Blight." The Major looked up from the photograph just long enough to wink at Spenser. "She's an interesting girl, I give you that." The Major had pearly white teeth: they must have cost him a fortune. "She's . . . compelling. I'll admit that I'm anxious to take her out for a try. But the money you're asking . . . suppose I gave you half?"

Blight smiled so sweetly.

The very wealthy, sandy-haired, blue-eyed Major beamed sincerely.

"Be reasonable, Blight. Only look at this realistically . . . why, for the amount you want for this . . . oh say, *this unusual girl,* I could buy any three beautiful waitresses in this club. *Three,* Blight. And real hot ones. And goosey as a man could want . . . !"

To illustrate some pointless point, the Major made a stab at the long, mesh-covered legs of one of the house beauties. She sidestepped him easily. The Major turned back to Blight, who was sipping an after-dinner cognac and waiting while the Major talked himself out of all his bargaining powers.

"Blight," the Major gushed. "Blight, I'm not saying that I don't want her. I do, Blight, I want her very much. I'm not trying to create any false impressions. My cards are on the table. . . " The little military rat did not deem it necessary to add that his cards were also up his sleeve, down his pants' leg, and under the table. The Major was a famous sportsman, and he carried his own cardtable, complete with his own marked cards. A stacked deck. He played a less than honest game. Curiously enough, no one but the Major ever lost.

Someone is always wrong, somewhere.

"Let's compromise." The Major didn't have a single original idea. He ordered them wholesale from Canada. "Tell you what. You come down a few dollars, and I'll go up a few. Meet you halfway there, Blight. How's that strike you?"

The Major's face had the grainy texture of dried beef. Blight preferred not to pinch his cheek. He contented himself with reaching over and tapping the Major's wrist significantly.

"Major, as one old horsetrader to another. . ." The Major's hand fled to his lap, and Blight started tying up the bag. Not salesmanship, but plain, old-fashioned tack-room tactics. "Major, my card is on the table too . . . in fact, it's in your hand. That picture . . . can only *suggest*. The rest I leave to your imagination."

" . . . put her over the jumps," the Major was telling himself. He couldn't stop thinking in terms of cavalry.

" . . . for a great deal of money, you may be sure. You might even say, an *indecent* sum of money," Blight was saying it. "However, the price in-includes buggy whips, special bits, blinders, a black mesh feedbag that buckles on from behind, a genuine Palomino horsehair tail . . . you get a lot for your money, Major. Of course if you feel it's exorbitant. . . "

The Major gnawed at his pinkie. Katy's photograph brushed his lips. "Dear, O dear . . . a thoroughbred, eh Blight? Now, you're sure?"

"I'm positive! Just take a look at her mouth, Major. You know yourself that you can always tell a real thoroughbred by the size and shape of her mouth. And there, Major, take a good look at that mouth. See how tender, how it retains its natural shape. That's rare these days. This ponygirl has never had the bit between her teeth. You'd be the first . . . !"

"Really! Never taken the bit . . . !" The Major wasn't much of a horsetrader, actually. He didn't know it yet, but his price had just gone up two hundred dollars.

" 'Pon my word!" Blight blessed a thousand magickians, dead and burning. For them he said the old benediction. . . .

" . . . in a stable. Now I'm not saying that she's never been mounted. I don't take you for a complete fool, Major. But I am telling you that she's never been saddle-broke. She's never been put through her traces . . . well sir, it's been very pleasant." Blight plucked the photograph from the Major's sticky fingers.

"Here, Blight! I say, where are you going, man? We haven't finished discussing. . . "

"Yes we have, Major." Blight has the friendliest smile in America. "The price is the price and you're welcome to pay it. Or not. But I really must dash. . . ."

The Major scrambled to his feet and frantically signaled for a waitress. Since he was only four feet tall, almost everyone overlooked him. Naturally this didn't make him much less frantic.

"Here, wait a second, can't you? Where's that damned waitress! Blight! Where are you going?"

"To the stables. I've just gotten the urge to take a midnight trot. Come along . . . if you can raise the price, *plus*."

"What say?"

"If you're coming, better bring along a few extra hundred dollars, *for the incidentals*." Blight raised his arm and snapped his fingers, one time only. The three prettiest waitresses instantly appeared with silver bowls full of fresh carnations. Blight picked a red one and pinned it adroitly on the swelling bosom of the bustiest of the three. Then he plucked a black one for himself, turned smartly on one heel and went off, without looking back. Jaunty, and only a little bowlegged. . . .

"Here, Blight!" The Major gave up fumbling with his coin-purse. He threw a handful of twenty dollar bills on the table, emptied the sugar bowl into his pocket; and his jacket bulging with the sweet lumps, he galloped across the nightclub floor after Blight.

"*Tally-Ho!*" cried the three waitresses. But the Major, so magicked up that he could hear only his own hoofbeats, never realized that he had been perfectly correct. *He could have had the three prettiest ponies for the price he was rushing to pay for one!*

(one photograph)

Spenser, so to speak, was always bringing the boys home from the office, from the club, the neighborhood tavern, the bus-stop.

SURPRISE PARTIES ARE LOTS OF FUN! was Spenser's contention. And sometimes, to prove it, he'd stroll out for an afternoon promenade, and return with all sorts of queer chums. It might be a banker, or it might be a shoeshine boy: fifty cents or fifty dollars . . . people need more than bread to live. And certain people need more than other people need. Some people need a high protein diet, dangerous drugs, and outrageous games.

When Spenser stepped out for a casual constitutional, Katy had no way of knowing who would be coming back. By the same token, Spenser, rattling his key in the lock, returning from his stroll around town, never knew who was waiting; for Katy, a champion in the female class, had taken to greeting him (and his chance companions) in retaliatory postures that provoked the most stunning variety of reactions from Spenser and his many, many gangbang friends.

                "Hi-Ho, ducky, I'm home!" Spenser chortled cheerfully from the living room, one afternoon. "Brought an old school pal home with me, dear. He wants to meet you, dear. . . "

O dear.

The bedroom door was open just enough for the two men to see Katy from the waist up, in the bedroom, hanging from a silken noose. Her sweater was torn, and her face had turned black. Her tongue protruded from her twisted mouth.

Old school pals are the first to run; count on that. This one squawked and immediately vanished. Spenser just stood where he was and stared.

Katy winked.

Spenser pushed the bedroom door open all the way, and

found Katy's feet firmly planted on a chair. She laughed like a silver loon and tossed a burnt cork at him.

"Come on, Mister Bones, rub that on your red face and get into the act. Wouldn't you like to be as black as me?"

Spenser was close to being shocked. Katy was such a tricky lady. Her eyes were drawn down to dots.

"Katy! You've been into the medicine cabinet."

" 'Deed I have!" She stepped down from the chair and came toward Spenser, her noose dangling behind her. "I am a cup that now runneth over."

"You're an idiot who's just runneth a fifty dollar trick out her door," grumbled Spenser, a notoriously bad loser.

"Let him go, let him go. He hollered, so let him go. . . " Katy cadenced. Suicide always made her giddy. "By all means, let him go. We're well rid of him, that fellow. Did you see how he skipped? He must have a wonderfully guilty conscience."

Sometimes they played doubles. Sometimes rotation. Sometimes Katy would call the shots. Other times, it was Blight who had dealer's choice.

" . . . and I choose to tie you up before I go out this afternoon."

Their four-poster bed served the purpose. Katy was lying on her stomach while Spenser tied her, a limb to each post.

Now it's Blight, still top dog in this game, in this round. Blight on his knees beside the bed, flipping through a telephone directory. Yellow Pages. . . .

" . . . and I choose to call this number." He dials. Round and round the big-little wheel goes, where it stops. . . .

Who knows?

"Midnight Supply & TV Repair Service," a gruff male voice answered Blight's call. He held the receiver in front of Katy's lips. Her move.

"My television set isn't happening," she moaned a little as Spenser kneaded her flesh.

"You say your TV don't work?" the telephone voice horned back in.

"Yes, something like that," Katy murmured. There were certain conventional openings. "How would you like to send a man over, right away. Got some goodfellow there who might possibly know how to fix her up?"

"What did you say your address was, lady? I'll be there in ten minutes."

Katy, squirming on her stomach, told him where to come. "And I'll leave the door open in case I'm in the shower."

Click.

Spenser dialed the next number. Katy repeated her request for service.

"It's urgent," she breathed. "I hope you understand. . . "

"Lady, I'll run all the way." Three repairmen swore on the heads of their children.

" . . . so if nobody answers, just walk right in," Katy told the Voices-at-Large. Now she would get what she was asking for: now she would see the men she had been talking to.

Spenser made a last phonecall. A florist shop was nice enough to answer.

"Two dozen long-stemmed American Beauty roses, please. Have you a boy you can send them over with?"

"Certainly, sir. I'll send Johnny right out." (He's been waiting all his life for you to call.)

"Fine. The door will be open. Thankyou."

Click.

Spenser put the phone away. He took his overcoat out of the closet.

"But damn you, Spenser, what will I tell them?" Katy shrieked from the bed. "There's three repairmen and one messenger-boy on their way. What the hell am I going to say when they walk in here and find me . . . like this?"

"Never mind what *you'll* say . . . I just wonder what in hell *they're* going to say?" Spenser, pulling on his overcoat, offered no help.

"Don't go yet, Spenser. O give me a hint. What should I do when they all get here?"

Spenser, buttoning his overcoat. "Well . . . I suppose you could do something with the two dozen roses. But be careful of the thorns. They could make you bleed . . . which might be a good way to break the ice." He walked over to the bed, let her have a pinch of his snuff.

"I'd better be going now, love."

"Mmmmmmm." Katy sneezed elegantly. He could tell from the depth of her eyes that she was preparing herself, laying her plans. He left without disturbing her, pausing only for an instant at the foot of the bed. An electrical switch, disguised as an electric blanket control, turned on the Bergan tape recorder that was so cleverly concealed in the bottom of the bed. The same switch also activated the photoelectric eye that watched the bedroom door. Any person entering the bedroom automatically triggered the eye and set three Nippon spy cameras (two for motion pictures and one for stills) hidden at viewing points around the room (two in the walls and one on the ceiling), grinding silently, filming in secret, a secret.

Tape recorder, electric eye, cameras . . . this elaborate circuit of peeking gadgetry had been installed, in gratitude, by last week's repairmen. And had been received, the week before that, in payment for services rendered to the sales manager of a Secret Service company.

With a cheery, "Ta-ta, love!" Blight left the apartment without a qualm, and confident that he wouldn't be missing a thing. Except of course Katy. But that was the chance that they kept taking, everytime. . . .

Everytime that Spenser left without locking the door behind him.

And sometimes, when he entered without knocking.

And sometimes, someone entered behind him.

A gentleman, very tall, very thin, pallid, and dressed all in black. Black bowler, which he didn't remove; black gloves, he kept these on, too. Black overcoat, buttoned to the neck. An umbrella hooked onto his forearm. All very black. Perfectly correct. Except for the man's muddy rubbers.

Why muddy rubbers on such a sunny afternoon?

One of those questions that almost never are asked. Not when Katy's dressed to have a fit. Not when it's her turn to be surprising, does anyone ask about muddy rubbers.

Spenser didn't see her for a second, and then when he did see her, he wasn't sure that he recognized her. And if he did recognize her, then he wasn't sure that he believed his eyes.

Why was she standing in the corner of the room, stripped to her penitent's striped panties and monkey-skin bra? Who had put a four-foot dunce cap on her dark head, and drawn a phallus on her naked back, with a shade of lipstick that Katy *never* used.

Who? How? Why . . . ?

"Because I've been a naughty girl," Katy lisped over her shoulder. But that was hardly an explanation. It was simply an excuse to flaunt her buttocks . . . the excuse as transparent as the material that covered them. Not that anyone had objected. Until just now. . . .

"This is Edhardt," Spenser said sadly. "Edhardt is an old friend of the family. . ."

"She was supposed to be just like dead," Edhardt whined.

"Didn't you make me a promise she would be dead? You said, *dead*. You said, *still*. You said that she would be laid out among the stinking lilies. That's what you promised . . . and it wasn't true!" Edhardt's reproach was so terribly sour that Blight couldn't help puckering.

Neither could he help Katy's current affectation, any more than he could explain it.

Katy continued in the corner, face to the wall. A model child, being punished. For something.

But Edhardt didn't care about that. He stood on Blight's promise. He stood and waited: hatted, gloved, prissily umbrella'd, and rubbered.

Katy didn't have to turn around to know that he was staring at her. She could feel his eyes scorning her naked backside, her decorations, her burning flesh, alive, alive-O.

       "I wanted her *dead*. Stiff! Dead! That was the arrangement." Mean, mean. Edhardt was mean. His voice made Katy's skin crawl. She kept her nose stuck in the corner.

"If she's going to be alive, who wants her? No. You said, *dead* . . ."

Is Blight dead?

    Not on your life! He is a modern master, a great crowd-pleaser. Just when you think that he's going to lose, that's when he gets you from behind.

He grabbed Katy by the back of her neck. She'd never even heard him approach.

"Yes, I said, *dead!* Don't doubt my word, Edhardt. I promised you the best dead you ever had. That means, *Fresh Killed!* It's the only way. Kill them right in front of your eyes. That way you know what you're getting . . . " Blight put his other hand around Katy's neck. He pressed her face against the wall.

Edhardt had a nervous giggle. "How do you mean that?

That is, what do you mean? I mean, what are you going to do to her?"

"*Dead*, said I. I said it!" Blight muttered grimly. His knuckles turned white as he whispered, "Never would I break my word, my bond, my blight! Her neck first . . . " he grunted. His knuckles grew even whiter. The vein in the center of his forehead stood out, purple with fury: pulsating violently, but silently. Hooded rage or vasoconstriction?

Blight never answers ambiguous questions. What he does is make bigger, better promises.

"What I'm going to give you will be even better than I promised." He promised Edhardt, who had come seven shy steps closer. Come, in fact, almost as far as Spenser's side; real close to Katy. . . .

She felt Spenser's hands and Edhardt's umbrella. Heard the Blightstrüm raving over her head.

" . . . not only are you getting a woman who is dead, but I am presenting you with the rare opportunity of watching that very woman die! Or are you asleep? Don't you realize what you are getting . . . ?"

GETTING ANY?
Do you get enough of what every man craves?
Romance missing?
You can get it in a plain, sealed envelope.
Get it!
Try

FASCINATION, a guessing game. Any number can play.
" . . . Katy, honey, are you decent?" Spenser called from the living room.

"Hi, honey. Is that you?" Katy's voice came from the bathroom. "I've been in here all day, waiting for you to get home."

"Say, puss-cat, I've brought a friend home with me . . . " Blight called.

"Say, lover, did you remember to bring home the cold cuts?" Katy called back.

Spenser turned to his friend and winked. "She can't hear a thing we're saying, not with that bathroom door closed. Would you believe it, the walls in this apartment are 36 inches thick. And that's a fact."

"Come on, lambie!" Katy was in excellent voice this afternoon. She was piercing in many different registers. "Toddle in here," she trilled. "Come kiss me where . . . "

"WHOOPS!" Spenser bellowed, drowning out the rest of her words. He nudged his newfound friend. "She's a great little girl," he told this fool, the one that had followed him home this time. A beefy, coarse-grained, expensively dressed lummox . . . where in the world does Blight find them?

" . . . great sense of humor!" Spenser slapped his pal on the back. "Listen, how'd you like to surprise her silly? Listen, I've got an idea . . . you're not the bashful type, are you?"

The lummox showed his crocodile teeth: he shook his thick head. "Not me, buddy, not me. I'm game for anything you got in mind. . . "

In spite of the walls, three foot thick, Blight lowered his voice. " . . . doesn't know that you're here," he was telling his big-shouldered, pigeon-chested, ten-minute acquaintance what would be fun, when Katy's voice cried urgently,

"OH! HELP! COME QUICK! I've got soap in my eye! Bring me a towel . . . O hurry hurry hurry!"

"Go get her!" Spenser fired from the hip. The lummox thundered across the living room: permission granted, he ran for the sweet tart, who called out from the bathroom.

"O bring me something to wipe my eye . . . !"

The bathroom doorknob came off in the big bear's paw.

"What should I do now? It broke . . . " He held the door-knob up for proof.

"The door isn't closed. Just lean on it and it'll open.

.

.

.

. . . . but .

.

.

be careful . . . !"

It seemed a little late to shout after the ox had hurled his own brute weight against the unlatched door.

Which flew open. And the momentum of his charge almost carried him into the tub. Only the shock of what was in that tub stopped him in midair.

Just Katy, sitting there breast high in bubbles and soapy green water. Just Katy, dressed for church, and taking a bath. White hat on her head; her face perky and sweet and mysterious under a brown veil; respectable pink and white dress; long, white gloves . . . and, although the soapy water obscured the rest, Spenser had not the slightest doubt that she had not neglected to wear hose, and her high heels and. . . .

But certain things need not be discussed. So Spenser and Katy merely exchanged conjugal kisses and ignored the Lug, who was staring at the obvious.

"Katy, I'd like you to meet an old Marine buddy of mine. We used to do a lot of shooting together. Katy, Charles . . .

Charles, Katy."

Katy's dress, a sheer organza, soaking wet, clung to her pouting breasts; the soft brown aureoles showed plainly through the flimsy material. Her nipples, pointed.

"So glad to meet you. Spenser's told me so many nice things about you, Carl. . . . "

"Charles."

"Quite." She flicked him a cockeyed smile that made him forget that she wasn't supposed to be sitting in a bathtub with all her clothes on.

Ladies' breasts always made him passionate. And when lummoxes get passionate, they tend to forget a lot of things. Sometimes they forget so far as to address their betters in the familiar tense.

"Say, Spence, you old dog," Charlie was beginning to sweat. His kind always do. He pulled a fat handful of bills out of his pocket, counted off twenty of them, and handed them to Spenser. "How's about you hopping out for some beer and liverwurst? Like we were talking about, remember? Here, you take this and. . . "

"No. I'll take *this*." Blight picked the main wad from the successful bum's hand. The twenty bills went, rolled like a hollow wand, into the beefy boy's jacket pocket. "You may need it for carfare," Spenser insisted. And cut short any protests or expressions of gratitude, with his hand held up like a butcher's knife.

"Liverwurst comes high," was his last word on the subject. Charles looked pained. . . .

"Look at me," Katy laughed from the tub.

Casually flicking the spy switch ON, Spenser strolled out of the apartment. . . .

. . . Came back twenty-seven hours later to find the lights low, soft music on the phonograph, and Katy stretched out luxuriously on the plum-colored, plump, silk-covered divan.

"Nice place you got here," said the one he'd brought back

this time. "Real nice." The hayseeds were sticking out of his nose.

"Hi there, you." Katy stirred languorously. Yawned contentedly.

"Where's Charles?" Spenser couldn't help wondering. Katy pointed at the bathroom, and Blight went to look. Just as he'd suspected. . . .

Big Charlie, collapsed in the tub, knees drawn up to his chin, the green bathwater turned to brown scum, sloshing gently over his slumbering, fully clothed, prize hunk of a waterlogged body.

Which made it fifteen straight for Katy. Naturally Spenser doesn't mind. He stepped into the bedroom to check the automatic camera. Twenty-nine thousand feet of raw stock, Triple Flash Pan sees in the dark. Fifteen hundred feet of magnetic tape, listening under the bed. Reserve cans of film and tape . . . Blight rushed back to the living room.

Everything was alright. The Rube was still standing beside the divan, staring down at Katy. She was writhing, arching her back and rubbing her backside against the plump, silken cushions. And all the while her contortions grew more violent, but she made not a single sound. Only the scratchy, electric sound of silk rubbing on silk; and the heavy breathing of the petrified Ruben. Who just stood there, stretching his scrawny neck.

Three minutes, four . . . eventually Katy subsided. She lay very still, eyes wide open, her skin luminous. So much skin showing.

She was undressed in a garment that Spenser had never seen before. Odd, since he selected *all* of her clothes. He was positive that he knew every article in her wardrobe. . . . This was particularly attractive: a snatch of black panties fitted her rounded hips and full buttocks just as perfectly as skin. Delicate red stitching tied the brief together, weaving a pattern around her thighs.

Then Katy, without any warning, uncurled her long legs and rose like sea-spume thrown up between the rocks . . . Katy stood between Spenser and the stranger, and laughed to see their eyes pop.

They saw, both of them at the same time, that Katy's costume, bra, panties, dark hose, and crimson garter . . . *had been painted on!*

"Who wants to lick it off?"

"Who wants to go first?"

"Who painted it on you?" Blight can't be blamed for asking. But Katy was covered by the other man, the famished farmboy, the Rube with an anteater's tongue . . . obviously she was too busy at the moment to answer.

And then later, she forgot.

Later, she couldn't remember whether it had been latex rubber that she had been packed into, or whether she had been wrapped in rolled, wet skin . . . perhaps natural lambskin would do her a trick. Lambskin to cover the wolf of her heart. Under lambskin she could prowl the innocent flocks at her whimsy, and eat whom she chose. And who would suspect her?

She had the oval-shaped face of all the best and most beautiful Madonnas. . . .

". . . lick it off!"

And there's your bad Katy. Ravening, slathering; belted and booted according to every fashionable fetish. . . .

. . . booted and spurred, masked grotesquely, and savage as an Amazon. A vicious quirt dangled from the loop round her wrist. Strapped to her maiden's crotch, a monstrously large dildo; leather, spring-steel, and cunningly tipped with rubber. It wobbled with oversized menace, as she approached. . . .

"Somebody save me!" screamed Mimi, throwing himself face forward on the pillows.

Käi rearranged his legs for her convenience.

"Save me! Save me! Mistress gonna kill me!" screeched the new maid, having hysterics already.

Käi cut him smartly with her quirt. "Damn you, hold still!"

But Mimi paid no attention: he was too far gone into his own dream. "Save me!"

She lashed him again. "Damn you, I'm trying . . . !"

"Try harder, Horsey. You must try harder!" the Major urged, reaching for his long, leather-tongued, split-lash tickler.

He buckled on the head-harness and backed her between the aluminum shafts of a two-wheeled buggy. The Major had had it built, years before, at great expense, and to his increasing sorrow. What jockey wouldn't wince to see that darling, elaborate rig hitched to jades, hacks, plowhorses, nags, thick sluts . . . but what else was available at the horsetraders' mart?

Oh yes, once in a long, long while they might have some acned, knock-kneed, runaway virgin, fat around the ankles; but they'll call her a colt, and she'll fetch a fine price . . . for what?

The Major turned the problem over. Never had he harnessed a filly like Katy. A skittish beauty, she stood reluctantly between the shafts, while the Major fumbled, and finally clicked the shafts to the two metal rings hanging down on either side of her belt-cinch. Hardware.

"Haw there! Haw! Haw! Easy does it . . ."

Katy was shy of the bit. Shy. . . .

. . . the old Roughrider's face split into a broad grin. And he kept a firm grasp on her checkrein. And taunted her with the dreadful bit.

Katyap-Katyap, Hi-Ho Katy.

"So you've never taken it in your mouth before? Well here now, here's your chance to see it before you get it . . . Oh yes, you're going to get it. But first I want you to see it. Come on there, pet. I said, *look!*"

The Major was fair proud of that bit. He'd made it with his own hands, from his own design; taking a quarter-inch rod of stainless steel, which he covered with a piece of rubber tubing to avoid injuring the tender, unbroken mouth. The young, sweet mouth. . . .

The bit was shaped like a deep V, with a longish metal stud at its apex. "You may sniff it, old girl," the Major teased meanly, waving the nasty thing in her face. A stableman of some sixty-nine windbreaking years, the Major was receiving his trophy tonight. Who wouldn't be nervous? His legs were bandied and his boots were ugly and his breath made Katy think of frogs.

Katyhorse . . . she tossed her head this way and that, but, harnessed to the buggy-shafts, tied by her checkrein and nosechain to a whipping-post, the only defense she had against his bit was an ineffectual attempt to keep her jaws tightly closed. He'd sweat to make her open them. . . .

Not at all. He merely pinched her nostrils together, with one hand. . . .

She gasped for air, and the Major rammed the bit in, a bit harder than was necessary. Then, with a brutal jerk, he took in the slack on the chin-strap, and the bit was in place. The metal stud pressed down on her tongue, near the palate, making her gag, keeping her from speech. She could neigh, she could whinny, she could haw and she could whimper, but intelligible speech was denied her. The bit was a great success: she was exquisitely tongue-tied. And despite the rubber tubing, the V-bar hurt her mouth dreadfully. And not only that, but it also caused her to dribble, on account of which, she was terribly humiliated.

"Ready for a trot, hey?" (*Thwack-thwack*) The Major's quirt snickered. . . .

CUT.

Mimi was bleeding.

CUT.

The three automatic cameras continued to record the details at 120 frames per minute on 16 millimeter film . . . the tape recorder spun a long spool. Recording the event just to prove once again. . . .

CUT.

. . . that nearly everybody likes to have his or her picture taken with a dummy. And there is simply no adequate explanation for certain popular eccentricities. They are. More we may not say.

Trick photography only panders to the need. It unfortunately adds little to our comprehension. And even ponces tricky and as able as James Spenser Blight, by accident or design, occasionally prepare an overdose, and then we read something that seems to concern us in the morning newspapers. . . .

But how can we be sure?

The hand-me-down facts fit badly, if at all. The account is garbled, the names misspelled, the descriptions slanted, distorted, exaggerated to pander to the public's addiction to sensation, no matter how remote.

We have no idea of what really happened. We only know

that we stole a newspaper, one morning early, from the corner we-trust-you newsbox, and therein read an article of ancient history concerned with the mysterious death of a Belgian (French?) housemaid (lady's maid?) in the

swank Nob Hill apartment of a beautiful young photographer's model, Miss K. Knight, who has been missing since last Wednesday.

According to Capt. Adore of the S.F.P.F.'s Search & Seize Bureau, the official looting, which took place after the homicide, revealed a huge cache of evidence pointing to full-scale operation of a blackmail ring whose victims included some of the city's most prominent persons as well as known deviates and offenders.

In addition to fifteen address books, naming more than six score and ten clients, their phone numbers, prices, and preferences, Police have also turned up a total of some thirty-five hundred indecent photographs of Miss X and her many swains; mostly in the nude, but in some pictures, costumed in bizarre and suggestive outfits. In addition to the photos, more than twenty-five thousand feet of motion picture film, and what Police have characterized as a "significant" number of tape recordings of audio puerilia have been turned over to Official Laboratories for processing.

CLUELESS

"In spite of all the evidence, we don't have a thing to go on," a Public Relations officer told newsmen today. "All we've been able to establish is that the same woman posed for each photograph. But she always wore a wig and such a variety of fantastic masks that we haven't been able to identify her positively. She might be the lady who rented the apartment, she might be the Queen of Eurasia. we just can't bring ourselves to make a positive identification."

In other developments, the Bureau was able to deduce that the Sex Extortion Syndicate made most of its contacts through classified advertisements in local newspapers. Police cited one instance where a certain brand of raincoat was offered for sale. The ad was innocent enough, except to experienced perverts who recognized the brand name as a codeword for coitus.

The Cryptology Squad are examining sixteen shoeboxes packed full of "application" letters, from persons of every walk of life. Army officers, clergymen, lawyers, physicians, sportsmen, undertakers were among those who answered the classified advertisements. Some of these men were subsequently photographed with Miss X in compromising positions. Many more of the applicants were not invited to meet her, and weren't photographed. They were blackmailed anyway.

ROMANCE MISSING? ROMANCE MISSING? ROMANCE

IX

"Love seducing innocence, pleasure leading her on, and remorse following."

Such was the way of the world, the sword in the sky, the razor-edged tricks of the trade, the danger inherent in too diligent a devotion to the erotic muse.

Of course there was a cushy position waiting for him with the Post Office, any time he was ready to listen to reason and cease his exciting industries. They offered him all sorts of pensions and lots of life insurance, a full and honorable pardon . . . but Blight preferred to continue his passionate commissions, his investigations and experiments, et al. And to hell with threats from the walking dead, to hell with persecutions carried out by uniformed golems, paid assassins from the Doctors' Syndicate. They had all the machine guns on their side, and the mathematicians to prove that it was only a matter of time till they caught him, *so would James Spenser Blight please come down to the nearest Precinct house, and please, would he bring his wife along with him?*

No he wouldn't. Blight refused. He categorically refused to cooperate. And they couldn't frighten him, neither could they bribe him, and slowly they began to realize that there wasn't a hope in hell of diverting him from the Mysteries and his vice, his habit, his vending, his only source of income.

Now they began to hate him in earnest, and the way they would say his name was so nasty it made their dogs snarl. And because he wouldn't work for them, the Post Office took to pinning up his picture, offering rewards to any Judas-minded citizen who would come forth with information leading to the capture and conviction of that poisoned apple, Blight, James S.

Blight laughed to see the dogs barking up all the wrong

177

trees, arresting all the wrong people, while he went right on with his work, his chosen occupation, went on evoking venal apparitions. He went on celebrating his magick, acting as his own Apothecary: a practicing Psychopomp, a Naturist, a Deputy and a Gentleman. So he styled himself on letterheads and printed notices.

!!!ATTENTION!!!

A BEAUTIFUL CRAZY will be Performed on Wednesday next, at eight o'clock in the evening, at the How Towne Grange Hall Post #909, by a Magister de Deceptio, and his White Witch. OR A FANCY BEAUTIFUL, a Practical Demonstration of a Long, Elegant, Silver Curve. One Dollar ($1.00) will be Charged at the door. A Lecture with Lantern Slides, a Song & Dance and

an opportunity to purchase a subtle and effective aphrodisiac, developed by an ancient physician, rediscovered by Blight, after being lost for centuries, now bottled and labeled, but not yet patented under the trade name of Blight's Own Elixir, or Extract of Sweetarts ("Bite 'em for a burst of flavor!"); or ask for it by its genetic name, Sadducismus Triumphatus. Ask Blight, because he's the only chemist who can make it: only Blight has the formula, an infallible method for bringing the maid around, by means of an odorless, tasteless, colorful modicum of blue, green, yellow, red ingredients, soluble. And priced for popular consumption.

*********XTRA ATTRACTION*********

Appearing on the Same Platform:

*K*A*T*Y*

the Lady with the Magnopathic Hands
Invites
Cripples, Chronic Invalids, and Persons who
Suffer from Curious and Intimate Ailments,
May Apply for Secret Consultations. A Warm
Touch May Help You 2

Was that a crime? Just exactly whom were they hurting, traveling around the state in a faded blue Plymouth station wagon; bringing their entertainments to outlying areas, remote communities badly in need of fun and new games? So what if they lectured at civic club meetings, small-town firehouses, highschool auditoriums, in clapboard motels and at county fairs? And why should anyone care if they did baptize a bumpkin or seven; we all get carried away by ourselves. Grant that Blight did transplant more than one farmer's daughter from her native soil to more rarefied dirt. Was that really so wrong? If so, Blight's sorry. His intentions are sterling, his chemicals unadulterated. He scrubbed his hands at least ten times a day; his instruments were sterilized according to prescribed and time-hallowed ritual. Nobody ever caught hepatitis from Blight. So even if he did do a little dispensing, why should a large soft drink company hate him like poison? Didn't Blight enjoy enough enemies already? Since when has a formal education counted for more than zeal, consecration and the impassioned desire to do miracles? Self-taught, but sincere. Anybody can make a mistake, every recipe is fallible; why blame Blight because sometimes an error is forever? He's as sorry as everyone else.

Maybe sorrier.

After all, who was it that lost his whole head of hair, his

eyebrows, his quicksilver physique, all in the holocaust of a single afternoon? Blight blew his beauty and grace and brought on his glandular misfortune by the merest miscalculation. Read 0.00025 for 0.0025, or read it the other way around . . . it's only human to forget which way you are facing . . . and you too can expand your proportions. But it's a trick that can be done one time only.

"It won't work," said Katy, sitting on a stool in the corner of Spenser's laboratory, pretending to knit but actually watching his every move. "It simply won't work the way you're doing it."

"And why won't it work?" Blight went on stirring the fluid bubbling in the distilling flask. In scientific matters, Katy is perfectly faithless. "Why won't it work?"

"Because your mechanics are wrong."

The liquid turned bright orange, hissing in the flask. Spenser lowered the flame under the glass, and the orange ran red as blood.

"How do you know whether it's wrong or right?" Spenser asked, not unreasonably. "Katy, you haven't even seen the formula. How do you know what I'm doing?"

"I don't have to know," clickety-click-click went Katy's long steel needles. "All I have to do is look and I can see that the sediment isn't fluffing out properly. I told you that you should let it rise before you start diluting and stirring. Now you know that I said that, Spenser. You heard me say it." Katy's needles flashed in the white glare of the unshaded lightbulb.

Blight was watching the gray-green jelly solidifying in his pyrex flask. He turned the single-jet Bunsen burner as low as he dared: the green caste suddenly collected itself and leapt out of the flask in a plume of pale green smoke. "That's interesting . . ." muttered Blight, who would have done better to give Katy his attention. Instead, he drained the excess fluid off; drew it up through a cotton filter, and sniffed it with a cautious nose. It smelled of mulberry and patches of mint, and it had the good golden maple color of fermented cider.

"Perfect!" chortled Blight. "I've done it at last!"

"Not yet, you haven't," Katy kept on knitting. "You've still got a chance. Go squirt that slop into the toilet, and start afresh with a new batch . . ."

"Nonsense! This stuff is perfectly wholesome . . ."

"No it isn't, Spenser."

"We'll see . . ."

". . . Don't! Don't do it Spenser, don't . . . !"

"Well . . . there! I did!" Spenser straightened up; his eyes were receding back into his head. "You see, I did the whole tube-full and look at me. I feel fine . . ."

Ten minutes after one o'clock in the afternoon. At one-fifteen the first signs of the Amorata Syndrome appeared: fevers, sharp decline in the systolic pressure, hallucinations, excessive cerebral stimulation.

Blight was lying on the floor of his laboratory, his hands clasped behind his neck, his eyes tightly shut.

At two-o-five in the afternoon, Blight was neither sweating nor salivating; his rectal temperature was 109.9. He was delirious and unmercifully lucid. He was conscious but unable to control his psychomotor, a victim of his own runaway reflexes. Glossolalia relieved some of his tension, but it was horrible to have to lie there and listen to himself jabbering, babbling. . . . When Katy realized what was happening, she ran for her bones and her rattles and her drum, while Blight lay writhing, jerking and twisting and frothing at the mouth. He was still doing convulsions on the laboratory floor when she returned, breathless, her arms full of equipment. He rolled round the laboratory, or rather, *was rolled* in the throes of impulsive, high-frequency fits.

Better dead than Blight, paying for all his crimes at once; simultaneously speaking in several tongues, burning, bleeding, erupting, suffocating . . . Katy began her dance. Tapping her drum with her fingertips, she kept her own rhythm, the pacifying tempo of the Anti-spasmotica. Her metal-capped high heels made sparks fly around Blight, who gradually subsided.

The afternoon burnt itself down to regret; the mountains turned ugly and the oceans turned black. Gulls followed the fishing craft home, and the bay was blanketed with their sad gray wings. The tides rolled out and the wind fell off.

The auto traffic moved slowly over the bridges as the people fled from the city. Streetlamps went on, and the night closed in. Blight lay on the laboratory floor. Vastly altered. Katy sat on him, marveling greatly.

From that moment on, she was a confirmed Therapeutic.

As for Blight, the kindest description we can apply is merely to note that the picture of him hanging in all the post offices no longer was valid. Amen.

2.   Somus, the gentle dreamer, was often evoked to send his son Morpheus, the counterfeiter of dreams, to ease Blight's plight in the anguished months following that afternoon.

Katy had saved him but, the crisis past, she couldn't go on succoring him indefinitely. Her curatives were limited— she was flesh after all—and in addition to Blight, she had taken to treating the sickness-at-large. And her patients came from all over the world.

She was already famous when Marlene Groz, the watercolorist, executed her oft-imitated *Katy Contemplating the*

Baron's Bald Head, and a whole host of art-lovers wrote in for appointments.

Gradually Blight grew accustomed to his new appearance. He started smoking cigars, rarely buttoned his pants, indulging himself in fat men's small ironic amusements. He rarely left his rooms, but would rumble around in a torn silk dressing gown, yards of rubber tubing trailing behind him. Katy had to work day and night to pay for his pastimes, his pleasures, his new triple tolerance. She accepted it as her new lot, and bent her back to accommodate his load without complaint.

Out of gratitude, Blight dubbed her, better than a mother, his Mascot, his dark-tressed Champion, his Wife and Friend.

She thanked him and kissed him and hurried off to her next seance. Her days and nights were filled with consultations, massages, virility treatments, colonics, laying on of hands (her hands). . . . But for *that,* she charged extra. Her critics claimed, extortion. But they were distorting, exaggerating, selling more newspapers.

And still, despite their worst excesses, Katy continued to make more money than most of her enemies. A fatal mistake in these corrupt and jealous times.

A charge of mental poisoning was added to her already impressive Index, accumulating in the file cabinets of Central Secrets.

Lies, libels, myths, a modicum of fact, a great deal of quoting out of context. And even if Excitantia *was* catching, its effects were hardly as deleterious as the harm done by doctors giving out so-called tranquilizers, making up philters to curb the appetite, meddling in the chemical mystique, and then blaming Blight for their mistakes.

Yes, Blight! Or who do you think would suffer if Katy got caught? Who do you think they were *really* after? Whose head would they nail to the station-house door? Katy would get off with a warning and a kiss, but Blight they wanted for experimental purposes: *medical research* was the official phrase.

Doing good without a license was the true cause of complaint, and their snares were cunning and altogether despicable.

Blight stayed out of sight, even though there wasn't a chance that they'd recognize him; it was simply that he had grown weary of people. He let Katy commit the act on her own. Once in a long while he might peek through the keyhole, but they never changed the film. Katy always came in on cue; patients paid, spoke of their troubles. Katy listened till their time was up. Then she told them, got slapped, said Thank you, got dressed, called a cab, kissed her client goodnight and was gone.

Why should Blight bother to watch *that* again, every day, every night? Anytime he wanted to know what was happening, all he need do was open her purse and ask the money he found there. Hundred dollar bills folded into articulate little green squares, twenties and fifties folded less exactly, fives, tens, single dollar bills and loose change, crumpled indifferently, together with a damp hankie, a hairpin, other feminine accouterments at the bottom of her purse.

And then, one afternoon, he found a subtly worded invitation for Katy to come and explain and demonstrate her talents in front of a ruling body of doctors on such and such a day, at a place called Mother's Spa. Blight investigated and discovered that this was the State's brand-new mental penitentiary, a model institution where the patients regularly lectured the staff.

Katy had purchased a new hat for the occasion and she was dreadfully upset because Spenser refused to let her attend. She accused him of seeing ghosts in his bed, called him a fat coward, and told him to get more exercise.

"Spenser, you're becoming absolutely morbid!" She turned

over a dish of fine-combed powders; then locked herself into the bathroom for an eight-hour sulk.

Similarly she pooh-poohed the Warrant of Outrage, slipped under their door, one morning so early. The government bounty hunters never sleep. Spenser sighed and started packing. They would move at once, naturally.

But Katy, that prize innocent, slipped out to make one last house-call, confident that dark glasses were sufficient disguise.

She completely underestimated the extent of her popularity. A hospital agent saw her climb on the cable car at Market and Majik: five stops later, at Powell and Chestnut, an ambulance pulled up just as the cable car came to a halt. Two doctors, both very trim, wearing white coats and carrying little black bags, climbed on. One of the doctors, a willowy blonde, made up to the conductor, while the brunette made for Katy. In the ambulance, behind the wheel, a thickset woman, short iron-gray hair, broken nose, a tough, trained orderly brought along just in case. . . .

"... But I know a basically good girl like you isn't going to make a fuss. Why splinter those nice long fingernails and spoil your pretty puss when the end result is bound to be the same?" The brunette had a straightforward, sensible, social worker's approach. She put her hand on Katy's leg.

Katy looked at the hand and smiled. "I'd like to know where you think you're going to take me? If you don't mind my asking . . ."

The burly matron stirred at the delay. Katy immediately got to her feet. "O do call her off," she cried as the thick woman started to get out of the ambulance. Katy'd had so much experience with that type: short, thickset, heavy jowled, heavy muscled, baggy-bosomed turnkeys. She knew better than to make their job more interesting.

"Alright, Mary, we won't be needing you," the brunette doctor waved the thugress away. "Baby is going to be nice. Step down, sweets, step down." She helped Katy off the cable car. "Good girls get to ride up front, instead of riding chained in the back. See, it pays to cooperate . . . in you go!" She patted Katy's backside as Katy climbed in beside hairy Mary. "Come on, Marcia, we're ready to roll!" she called out to the blonde, who was having quite a chat with the coal-black conductor. "Marcia . . . ! Let's go, hon! I've got the woman . . . for Chris' sake, Marcia, you're lousing up our schedule!"

The blonde swung off the cable car just as it began to move. The conductor waved; she blew him a kiss, and then slid into the front seat next to Katy. The brunette got in last, slammed the door, and they drove off. The matron hit the siren and they wheeled through the early afternoon traffic, Mary's hard thigh pressing harder than was necessary against Katy's finely molded limbs.

"Cigarette?" the brunette doctor reached across the blonde to offer Katy a smoke from her pack.

"Thank you," Katy preferred her own brand but thought it more politic to accept. "If you'd just tell me where you're taking me . . . ?"

A match flared; this time it was Katy who leaned across to get a light from the brunette doctor's hand. "We're just going down for a little R.E. . . ." Her tone was less than credible. The blonde, in between, said nothing, only smiled and looked straight ahead. The matron was occupied with driving, and the confusions occasioned by her siren. That Marcia, so damned smug!

"Alright," Katy blew the smoke from her cigarette straight into the blonde doctor's bland face. "O I'm so sorry . . ." she drawled insincerely. Even Katy, that mild dove, may be driven too far.

"Just how far do you intend to drive me? And just what is this R.E.?"

"A Regular Examination, that's all, dear. No need to turn all nasty . . . we like you." The brunette doctor was unable to meet Katy's eye. She tried again to pass it on to the blonde. "Isn't that right, Marcia? Doesn't R.E. mean Regular Examination?"

But the blonde doctor, her eyes still tearing from Katy's smoke, only stuck her tongue out meanly. "Wait till you see *how* we examine you," she hissed. Katy had made another friend. "We're going to cut you open and see what's inside you. I'm really dying to get a peek at your ticking . . ."

The brunette doctor giggled, "Marcia, now you stop . . ."

"I'm going to shove my arm up to here . . ."

"Marcia! I want you to stop at once. Now she may be your meat, but just remember that she's *my* patient. And I will not have you upsetting her! As long as she cooperates . . ."

"Save it, bitch." Katy sat back; her eyes glazed, her heart sank. She recognized their insignia, their black and gold armbands. And now she understood their game; understood why she sat in the middle. Now there was no longer any need to ask where they were taking her. She'd been there before . . . this is what came of disobeying Spenser. Because he'd grown fat, she'd lost her faith; and now she was going for a ride. Katy cursed God and tossed the lit cigarette into the blonde's narrow lap. She was no longer cooperating.

And so tough Mary got her licks in after all. Katy rode the rest of the way well-shackled in the back.

They held her for a week—time enough for her bruises to heal. That was the degree of their cuteness. Detained for a week, incommunicado; they kept her all locked up in a rose-covered cottage near Los Gatos, some forty-five miles southeast of the city. During that week, she was kept trussed up in one room. She heard many voices, but the only person she saw was an old man, seventy at least, who came thrice a day to feed and water her. His words were always identical: "Hello, birdie," he'd greet her brightly, and bend to check that her knots were still tight. He had moss on his breath and his eyes glittered—Katy could see into his head; it was stuffed full of broken, jagged things. Toys chopped up small, and cracked baby birds . . . Katy only looked once. And morning, noon, and midnight, the whole long dreary week, he appeared with her pan, chirping the same senile tune.

"Sing for your supper, birdie," was all that he'd tell her, and then he'd never even wait for Katy to lullaby him, but, having spoken his sentence, he would flee the room. And this went on for seven days. Then came the final midnight, and Katy woke up screaming into a rubber cup that someone was holding over her nose and mouth. She gasped for breath and tasted the gas, but, just before she slipped under, she thought she felt long blonde hair brush her cheek. It was one of those mysteries: how could she ever be sure?

So delicately did they make their conspiracy. Phase the Second was precisely carried out, and Katy, unconscious, was transported to the city. They put her right back at the corner of Chestnut and Powell, deserted in the drizzle of 4:00 A.M., and there they left her, propped up against a lamppost, magicked right out of her mind.

And that's how the Garbage Company found her, half an hour later. Only try to imagine their surprise . . . naturally, they wanted to keep her.

Not until noon of the next day did they report her existence, and they did that by second-class mail; meanwhile she was held, better said, squeezed, in their sweaty custody, locked up in a tool shed, pending decision on a Scavenger's Writ.

Luckily for Katy, it wasn't granted, and her possession

reverted to the State Health and Maximum Security Hospital for Ladies. There she was given a Forever Classification Number, tattooed in blue numerals on her left forearm. She was *theirs* now, they argued, and wrote new laws to support their illicit contentions. What they did want her for, *that* they never did say. But no one may doubt that they surely would have gotten her . . . the fact that they had her confirms this conviction.

But, once in a very long while, the lights go out, the barn bursts into flames, the tables get turned: the Banque de Monte Carlo goes bankrupt . . . some state stooge gets a little too cute and files a Formality, not quite standard, and the deviation-hungry press seizes on the tidbit.

The next morning, the secret is out.

STATE FILES NOVEL BRIEF PROCEEDINGS AGAINST FEMALE CRAZY

"She is ours!" said Government Prosecutor J. J. Hungree at the Show-cause Inquiry now in Special Sessions. Hungree brought out the niceties of his legal machinations in the Sky-bar Room of the Federal Law Building yesterday noontime, shortly after submitting his tour de force to Circuit Judge A. A. Axelrod, Jr.

The petition read in part: "Because the Plaintive, the female found on a street corner, when questioned by professional physicians, was unable to satisfy the Vital Statistics Requirements; was unable to give more than her name, her shoe size, her age—two out of three answers which could not be substantiated—and the remaining 29 Basic Queries were not answered at all. She had no idea of the day of the month, nor of the Mayor of the City, no not even the Motto of the State could she recite, so little control had she over her own faculties. While, on the other hand, the State is in very nearly complete possession. Nine-Tenths of all Law is writ in our favor; ipso facto, the Right of the State is guaranteed. So confident that our Justice must Triumph, we swear to these statements, and to the truth of which we do affix our token signature, our Great Seal, and the brave slogan of our State: 'Alis Volat Propriis—She Flies With Her Own Wings.' "

"And that's right out of the Booke," Att. Hungree assured newsmen attending his luncheon. "If you don't believe me, you can look for yourself."

See Box on Back Page

Spenser's hands were shaking as he turned the newspaper over. . . .

Judge Axelrod, Jr., acting in consort with a Court-Appointed Sentencing-Doctor, handed down an Incarceration Judgment, favoring the State with its four hundred and fourth consecutive court victory.

Minimizing the influence of Persecutor Hungree's flukish plea, Axelrod, Jr., explained that his decision had come from his heart. Without a trace of a smile, the black-hooded Judge told reporters, "I examined the Creature-in-Question myself, and I am wholly convinced that rehabilitation is impossible in this case."

"Yes, Governor, that's what I said," Judge Axelrod, Jr., trusted his physical senses once too often; now he was acting under the impression that the Head of the State was talking to him on the phone.

At the other end of the wire, Blight barked in a voice not his own, "Details, your Honor, damn you! Details! What's wrong with her? What are they doing to her? What did she say when you spoke to her? Speak me the facts, d'you hear me? I want facts!"

Judge Axelrod, Jr., sighed and loosened his tie. He was alone in his private, crepe-draped chambers, but he kept his voice down to a whisper; by such silly devices did he hope to impress his Excellency the Governor. . . .

"Sir, the facts are unspeakable. Please believe me, it would only make you weep were I to tell you how unregenerate and wholly carnal she is, this vile woman . . ."

Blight chewed his cigar, waited for the fool to get to the point.

". . . Suffice it to say that after less than an hour, I was forced to terminate my examinations, so sickened was I by her candid admissions of practices so revolting that only a profound nervous disorder, that, or an Act of Demonic Possession, could possibly account for them. In either case, she's better off in a hospital . . ."

"Which hospital?" a voice very much like the Governor's demanded. "Name of Highest Bidder . . . ?"

"Las Lunitas, bid first, second, and third," the Judge automatically responded in the jingo of corruption. And his soul sank within him. He was sure that the Governor was asking for a present. "It was an open auction," he wheedled, he lied. "But there wasn't much interest. The regular buyers were mostly out of town. To tell you the holy truth, Your Grace, we barely covered court costs. Of course, I'll be making my usual donation . . ." sniveled Axelrod, Jr., into the receiver, the color of his heart, whispering his prayers into the mouthpiece, and his own dreadful whine is his answer. Cut off, he's too dull to feel it yet. But only wait till he stops talking. . . .

Blight can't wait. He gathers himself together like a storm. He's been brewing for a month, now he knows which way to blow.

And not a moment too soon . . . they had just that morning shaved her head.

Las Lunitas, a privately endowed institution, operated for the benefit of the Female Division, had sixteen acres of fenced-off wilderness. It took Blight ten minutes to drive through the grounds.

Still a quarter of a mile from the building proper, he parked his car by the side of the dirt road, and went on foot, the better to sniff out the lay of the land. Despite his great girth, Blight can walk a tightwire; he can step so softly that the squirrels don't look up.

Have you seen the full moon sail across the black velvet skies? See Blight prowl the grounds like a puffball; a fatty so silent, a phantom avenger, he slips through the weir wood that borders the front lawn. Now he steps out on a remarkable scene, spread across the greensward, like a Sunday in the park. Hundreds of people, whole families of sightseers, sensation and curiosity seekers, a messy rabble, they picnic and frolic in full view of the dread towers, the battlements and flying buttresses of the castle wherein they keep the *lunáticas*.

A single turret, much higher than the others, went up to the clouds: a finger pointing straight at heaven.

"Don't be in such a big, fat hurry!" one of the louts, stripped to his fishy-white waist, sunning himself on the green apron of lawn, called out as Spenser thundered past.

"Where are you rushing to . . . or don't you know that they're burning witches in there?"

"Aye, and I'm off to visit your mother!" Spenser snarled over his shoulder, never breaking his stride.

The closer he came, the more numerous the gawkers. Some of them had climbed trees and crawled far out on the limbs in bold attempts to see into the second- and third-floor windows.

One ragman on his holiday pulled off his cap as Blight bundled by; apparently taking Spenser for an Official Importance, he cravenly asked if assistance were needed. "I'm a good man with a faggot and a pyre, Your Lordship. And I'll work cheap."

"Yes, I dare say you will," Blight crippled the willing, would-be executioner with a measure and a half of withering scorn. Then he made his way into the administration offices of the madhouse.

As one might have guessed, the authorities were not awfully anxious to part with a prize captive like Katy. All those loafers lounging outside at fifty cents a head, buying refreshments and souvenirs from the hospital commissary, attested to Katy's popularity. She was a stellar attraction, no doubt about that.

Blight wandered through the administration hallways, making his reasonable request in a diplomatic voice, accompanied by the appropriate gestures, but all he got for his courtesies was a rubber-stamp runaround. Secretaries shook their heads, and clerks brought him rare, complicated, and out-of-date forms to be filled out in triplicate and returned two weeks from next Wednesday, at Window B, if you please. . . .

"No." Blight drew dollar signs on every paper. "Not next Wednesday. *Now*." And he handed back the forms together with a small gratuity. "Whom must I see about buying her back?" That was the question he asked all the hot hands. . . .

They took his money and pointed, *that way*.

Many, many counterfeit dollars later, Blight came at last to the sanctum sanctorum, the plush lair of the Guardian-Physician. . . .

"Impossible," that august person pretended, when bearded by Blight.

"Give me back my wife."

"Impossible. The courts have transferred her to our custody."

"Then I demand that the courts reassign her. I want a full-scale review of her case."

"My dear fellow, it simply can't be done." The G.-P. made sympathetic clucking sounds. The major portion of his professional duties entailed refusing reasonable requests from the relatives and close friends of the inmates. The clucking sounds, the watery smile, the pale hands fluttering over the patient's file: these were the insincere parts of his professional pose, his professional protection.

But James Spenser Blight was also a professional.

He appeared to be listening, O so attentively, while the physician described the state diagnosis and the reasons why they had to keep her.

"You see, the verdict was ignis fatuus or, in layman's terms, false light. Now until this condition is extinguished she'll have to abide with us. It's for her own good. I'm sure an intelligent fellow like yourself understands the necessity for isolating esthesiomaniacs from the rest of society. I'm certain that you understand. . . ."

"How much?" Blight understood the rules of ransom. But the Guardian-Physician insisted upon dickering.

"Now if this were just another Magick Nuisance charge, I could check the bail and bond schedule and tell you right off. However . . ." the physician's smile was buttered with imitation regret, artificially colored, preservatives added. "However, we've an exceptional number of complaints complicating this case, and . . ."

"What sort of complaints?" Spenser prolonged the interview. Mounted on the wall behind Doctor Duplicate was a floor plan of the asylum. Spenser memorized it while he feigned debate.

"Well . . . just for example, we have a letter here from a housewife in Sausalito, addressed to the District Commission and pleading . . . I say, would you like me to read part of it to you?"

"Please."

"Ah . . . yes. Here it is. I'll skip the first few pages and get to the heart of the problem. Now then, on page seven we have it. The Goodlady writes, and I quote:

> . . . apply for relief of your suffering subjects in Marin County, who groan under the threats and menaces of this sort of person, and who feel the effects of them everyday in the mortal, as well as the extraordinary maladies which attack us; in the reduction of affection usually tendered unto us by our husbands and lovers; as well as the surprising damage and loss of our material possessions. Further, more than one Decent Woman, residing in these parts, trying to protect her once happy home, has thereby incurred the implacable wrath of that Hussy, that Monsteress, that Sorceress, who vents her spleen on those who offend her by depriving them of aforementioned possessions, and, in addition, deprives them also of the faculties of speech, or the ability to play a game of cards.
>
> Sirrah, save us from this Scourge. On behalf of my Sex, in the name of my husband, and in the name of his husband, we pray you, *burn her!*
>
> Very truly yours,
>
> (Mrs.) Shirlee Umble

The physician slipped the letter into Katy's file again, but not so adroitly that Spenser couldn't see that the stapled sheets of paper were all blank.

"Then we have a telegram from the Union of Ordained Professors." Doctor Duplicate extracted a Western Union form from the manila file and blinked impishly. "You prefer me to read it to you?"

"O please do." Spenser was all reverence and wore the rapt expression of an Innocent, First Class. "O would you read it to me, please, yes, thankyou." He had nearly committed the blueprint to memory.

Doctor Duplicate cleared his throat and read in a loud, clear voice:

GENTLEMEN AND COLLEAGUES STOP
ARE WICKED SPIRITS MISLEADING THE
WORLD? STOP IS IT SUPERSTITIOUS TO
BELIEVE IN THE DEVIL? STOP BEWARE
THE SPELL. STOP STRONGLY URGE YOU
TO TAKE ACTION. STOP WHY NOT BURN
HER? CAN WE WATCH?

"Stop!" Blight interrupted the Guardian. He rose, the floor plan fixed firmly in his mind; he was anxious to be done with the niggling formalities. The sanctimonious stink of the G.-P.'s office, the stink of the physician himself, made Spenser's nose run.

"Just tell me how much you're asking for her," he said with no further pretense of politeness. "Your ears are dirty and your mail is black. Now, how much? Or do I make my offer to your superior? I'll make my payment in gold . . ."

"I'm certain you will," Doctor Duplicate bit off his words. His petty malice turned to rage as he realized that his visitor was cleverer than he was. "And your gold will turn green within a week. I know your kind, Mister . . . Blight! *Blight* . . . say, isn't that a Jewish name?"

"No," Blight answered softly. "It's a criminal name . . . and I wouldn't reach for that buzzer under your desk, Doctor. If I were you, I'd keep my hands right out where they can be seen."

Doctor Duplicate's face went yellow. His hands crawled back on top of his desk. His eyes bulged alarmingly. "That's a gun," he said. "What are you going to do with that gun . . . ? If you don't mind my asking," the doctor added hastily.

"Nothing to worry about, Doctor," Blight told him evenly. "You just keep your eye on the hole. *Keep looking at the little hole, Doctor.*"

The long, icy barrel of the Berrita .327 seemed to be

staring, reaching . . . the physician's jaw dropped. A tiny metronome inside the unwavering barrel began to click back and forth with a dreadful, measured, click-click-click. . . .

". . . click-click-click-click, keep watching the hole, Doctor." Blight suspended the Guardian-Physician's consciousness for the three minutes it took him to rifle Katy's file and discover which room she was locked in. Then Blight stripped the doctor of his white coat, disconnected the alarm buzzer under his desk, dragged the doctor into the closet where the file cabinets were kept, locked the closet door, and swallowed the key.

The time was 3:45 in the afternoon. Blight calculated that he had, at the outside, ten minutes to accomplish the impossible. He picked up the G.-P.'s little black bag, and left the ground-floor office through the open window.

And reentered the institution through the side door, the emergency entrance, at 3:48.

They were holding Katy in the Red Tower Suite. Blight climbed the iron steps, two at a time, and reached the red door at exactly 3:50.

He banged on the brass door till his knuckles bled, but no one came. The sound of his frantic rapping was soft and squishy. Altogether unsatisfactory. Blight turned away from the door, and lifting his foot after the fashion of great mules, he delivered such a kick that the metal sang like a cathedral bell.

The heavy portal swung back a quarter-inch. A mean red-nose poked out suspiciously. "Say what you want . . . *Here!* You can't come in here!" the crone croaked, too late. Blight had flung the brass door open, entering boldly, by authority of his white coat and little black bag.

"Who are you?" the old woman whimpered painfully,

rubbing her aching shoulder where the door had struck her. "Who are you, sir?"

"I am a Common Pricker of Witches," Blight answered in a lofty voice. "Where is she, the one who needs be trialed?"

The red-nose pointed to a sturdy oaken door. Fearing the Witch-Finder's eye, the hag covered her face with her shawl. "There, sir. She's in there. But you mayn't go in . . . the doctors are examining her . . ."

They certainly were.

Katy lay strapped to the operating table. Six doctors, wearing lipstick, stood around her, poking her with electric prods and making viciously disinterested comments.

Blight advanced, calming his murderous impulses with the promise that electrocution is a two-way proposition.

The doctor with the longest prod was demonstrating an opinion, and Blight used the time to prepare his props. He transferred some objects from his jacket pocket to his little black bag.

". . . tender spines, that is interesting. Also the reflexes lost, the sensation lost, eventually the muscles became palsied. Then we increase the voltaic reactions, so . . . and as you can see, the reflexes increase, and the sensations increase, and now the temperature of the kitty rises above the temperature of the rest of the body. And now the bedsores appear . . ."

Evil wisps of smoke curled up from Katy's singed flesh. They had forced a tennis ball into her mouth, and she could only moan and make little strangulated sounds. But her gray eyes grew brighter as Blight elbowed his way into the circle of chippies.

"He is the Witch Pricker, come to tap the hussy!" the hag cried from the door. Blight's rude treatment had made her his ally. She conveniently presented his illusionary credentials. His Junker sneer and stinging accent did the rest.

The doctors overwhelmed him with their credulity.

"Oh, what's this for?"

"Is this a straight pin?"

"Is this Holy Water?"

"What do you use this silver star for . . . ?"

"Doctors! Doctors, if you please!" Blight had placed the little black bag on Katy's bare belly, and now he was rummaging around, naming some very curious instruments. "Skidding tongs, single-tipped tongs, grasping rivet, angle-jaw . . . ah yes, here we are."

A sigh went up from the gathering. Blight ceremoniously drew on the long, magnetic gloves. He snapped the little bag shut and lifted it off Katy's stomach. The doctors were eager as terriers. None of them had ever seen a Common Pricker of Witches demonstrate the loathsome skills of his concentration camp craft.

Katy was all but forgotten as they fawned on Blight. His wristwatch told him that it was now 3:54. Time was running out, but no one could have guessed it from Spenser's unruffled, unhasty, completely self-confident air. He drew a slim silver case from his breast pocket, selected a cigar, offered none to any of the six cigarette lighters that immediately ignited and reached out to light him up.

"Thank you," said Blight vaguely, cigar between his teeth. "Now to work . . ." His oddly gloved hands danced in the air and a packet of paper appeared in the palm of his right hand. The doctors applauded.

"Nothing!" snorted Blight. "You have seen *nothing*. Sleight of hand! Pah!" He broke the seal and began unfolding the packet. "Closer, please. Now I commence the first step. Those who wish to witness the minute movements of the cuticle when sliced by the filament, will need come a step closer. The action is nearly microscopic, you should know. Even a step closer, please . . ." Blight had turned so that his back was to Katy.

The packet unfolded into a single sheet of paper about fifteen inches wide, seventeen inches long, and of a queer, off-white color. Spenser held the sheet in front of him so that the doctors and one old hag could read the tiny words printed at the bottom of the page.

Seven nosy noses hung inches away from the paper, and they read:

FOR USE
In an ashtray as a practical joke!
In a Bar or Restaurant to get service!
In doing magick tricks that need a professional touch!
If touched with a match, lighted cigarette, or
ANY HOT OBJECT
THESE SHEETS WILL FLASH WILL FLASH WILL FLASH

The glowing tip of Blight's cigar touched the flash paper shield, and the sun burst from between his hands. The flash paper went up in a great, golden blaze.

Inframarine contact lenses saved Blight from the seared fate of the seven who had faced him and now stumbled blindly about the Red Tower operating room, wailing and cursing and clutching their overwhelmed eyes. Their eyes, burnt out by Blight, at 3:55.

By 3:58 Blight had Katy off the table. The white coat that he'd stolen from Doctor Duplicate hung a few inches above Katy's pretty knees. Buttoned to the neck, nobody could know that she was naked underneath. At 3:59.2 Spenser and Katy fled through the oaken door, through the brass door, down the iron, spiraling staircase, out through the side door, the emergency door, and across the yard of the inner courtyard of the endless institution. Before they were free of its grasping, suffocating environs, they needs must creep through the wards of starving patients, waiting their turn in the Educational Building. Silently, they pad down the aisles of beds. Katy has the black bag. Blight steers her from behind.

"Doctor . . ."

"Ah, Doctor . . ."

"Water, Doctor . . ."

"Are you my doctor . . . ?"

The demented, dying inmates stretched their feeble hands after Katy. She did not stop to touch them: there were far too many, and besides, what was the use? They were all going to the Martyrdom Chamber, no matter what anybody did. And Blight and Katy would go along with them if they didn't get out of Las Lunitas very soon . . . 4:02. How long before one of the seven in the tower recovered her sight and stumbled out to give the alarm? How long before the Physician-Guardian was found locked in his closet? How many seconds (for surely their margin had melted to seconds) had they left? Still, one mustn't run. Obvious flight excites suspicion and the very last thing that Blight wanted was anyone asking any questions.

"*Where are you going?*" A starched torso blocked their passage. Looking over Katy's shoulder, Blight read the inscription on the breastplate:

HIGH NURSE

"Who is in charge here?" Blight bellowed, thrusting Katy aside. ("One side, Doctor!") and confronting the giantess who, only a second before, had been confronting them. "Name?" Blight's face was more than twice its usual size, swollen with instant rage that took a great deal of starch out of the obstacle's bosom. "Name? I demand to have your name!"

"But what is wrong?" the female oaf fell back. "Why should you want my name?"

"You are in charge?" Blight looked up at the frightened

mare's head. "You are the cretin responsible for this situation?" Blight screwed it to her good. 4:05.

Then taped her wrists and ankles together and tossed her over the railing. The snake-pit patients started crawling for her even before she hit bottom.

Blight and Katy couldn't wait to watch. But they could imagine. If they got out of the asylum there would be time to imagine. . . .

At 4:07 they crouched to one side of an open door. On the other side, a lecture was going on. . . .

". . . this experiment, we take a pre-disciplined male and chain him to the Dominant Female. Nurse Nan Ninetimes, will you be so good as to stand in for our bully-girl . . . ?" There was the sound of students squirming in their seats, as the clack-clack of a pair of highheeled boots marched up the lecture room aisle, then the clank of iron chains. A feeble voice protesting in monosyllabic despair, "No . . . No . . . No . . ."

"Now!" Blight whispered in Katy's ear, and chancing that the classroom would be looking in the other direction, they made a dash past the open door.

And out another window, down a corridor, across the parade yard, around the cook-shed . . . then, the agonizing, overlong, narrow, entirely exposed walk past the kennels and the outdoor punishment cages.

"Don't let them sniff the fear on you," Spenser forced Katy to walk slower. "Don't disturb these animals," he warned her softly. Keeping his fingers crossed.

It worked like a charm. They glided out of the interminable halls of the lunatic asylum, and the tea gong had scarcely died away in the chill of the afternoon when they came to the last gate, the inside-outside gate. The final barrier. Not fifty yards away, they saw the forest, dark and waiting for them. Once they'd gained those labyrinth shadows, the tall and threatening pines, no hound in hell, or hanging posse on earth could catch them. Katy has friends with feathers, and eyes that see in the night. She has furry, four-legged friends with clever claws and wicked fangs and ways of tripping hunters so that they fall down and die in the underbrush; while their prey runs free . . . *once they reached the forest.*

"Your pass?"
The hooded guardsman stepped out of the guardhouse, his automatic rifle at the ready. Behind him, inside the little hut, another sadist hoisted his weapon.

Blight's smile couldn't be more disarming. "The pass . . . now where is that damned pass?" He certainly makes a great show of slapping his pockets, earnestly searching . . . but neither automatic rifle seems particularly impressed.

And what, we must wonder, will Blight pull out of his pocket this time? What trick will he shake out of his sleeve? Smoke powder hidden in a hollow heel? Or a handful of disappearing dust? Or has he a trick flower in his buttonhole . . . ? *Smell this, officer. Smell this pretty flower . . . ! and SQUIRT the smeller gets a shower, a snoutful of Xneopycn acid.* But what about the other man, watching distrustfully inside the shack?

Not even Blight can fool them all. Every bag is eventually emptied, and the time comes when Blight can only shrug, and mutter lamely, "Must have lost my bloody pass."

Now make miracles.

Of a sudden, Spenser realized that the guards were not watching his antics. True, their rifles continued to point at him, but their eyes were definitely aimed elsewhere. Their attention fixed on someone else. Did Blight have to turn his head to know that Katy, standing a few feet behind him, had unbuttoned the white coat and stood revealed in all her nudity. Venus in the sunset. . . .

The way the guards gaped, you'd think she was the first freak of nature they had ever seen.

Where do you go when the whole world is after you? Where do you go when you have two bald heads, a stolen white coat . . . ?

You go down to the end of town, down where the street lights aren't so bright.

If you're an artful dodger, running for your life, you make for the narrow, crooked backstreets, streets lined with doorways perfect for disappearing into when the patrol car passes, its headlights giving fair warning.

Skirting the main part of the city, Spenser and Katy kept to the railroad tracks. Followed by the shiny freight rails past the docks, past grim wooden buildings, some pulled down, some fallen down, some trembling in the evening breezes. Sidewalks kept ending in a rubble of bricks, smashed wine bottles, buses parked for the night. They picked their way carefully through the tumbled-down ghost streets, stepping over the bodies of bums dead and dying. Hands reached up from the gutters to catch at their legs. Alley cats watched them with knowing, backstreet eyes.

They aren't the first fugitives to run this way. The old cats see them come, night after night, all night long. They run on the wind, their footsteps ring hollow on the secret backstreet sidewalks . . . down where the lights are not so bright, and nobody expects you to give your right name. Nobody expects you to explain. . . .

A snuff-colored moon, in its final quarter, hung upside down over the Travelers Hotel as Spenser and Katy came around the corner. The fog lay heavy in this part of the city.

It came up from the pavement. It swirled around their legs.

"In here . . ." Spenser said, and they pushed through the revolving door, into the lobby, the cave of echoes.

Now they are crossing the ocean of carpets, they pass beneath the arches, beneath the dusty, mammoth chandeliers. Now the shadows reach like long dark fingers across the huge and empty lobby. Now the shadows fall over them like waterfalls, now like dark moths.

Dead furniture. The smell of mildew, rubber plants, vague intimations of depravity, and dawn. . . .

The Nightclerk puts his book away. His custom-built, oversized swivel chair squeals as he heaves himself up. The floor is covered with bits of paper, parts of pictures, pretty-girl cutups. Gray stubble sprouts on the Nightclerk's fat cheeks, his eyes are red-rimmed, drawn back in his head. He blinks, his eyes tear. It's an effort to refocus.

"Damn you, Blight," he grumbled and stumbled past. "You're late again," said Blight, sinking back into his foam rubber, leather-cushioned, well-padded swivel chair. He sighed like a man all used up.